WITCHES, MURDERS

Paisley Island Cozy Mysteries Book 1

SCARLETT MOSS

HUMMINGWORD
PRESS

Copyright © 2023 by Scarlett Braden Moss
All rights reserved.
No part of this publication may be reproduced, distributed, or transmitted in any form or by any means, including photocopying, recording, or other electronic or mechanical methods, without the prior written permission of the publisher, except as permitted by U.S. copyright law. For permission requests, contact Scarlett@Scarlettbraden.com.
The story, all names, characters, and incidents portrayed in this production are fictitious. No identification with actual persons (living or deceased), places, buildings, and products are intended or should be inferred.

Book Cover by Elizabeth Mackey Graphics
https://www.elizabethmackeygraphics.com/

First edition 2023

Chapter One	1
Chapter Two	7
Chapter Three	13
Chapter Four	25
Chapter Five	33
Chapter Six	39
Chapter Seven	47
Chapter Eight	57
Chapter Nine	65
Chapter Ten	75
Chapter Eleven	83
Chapter Twelve	91
Chapter Thirteen	103
Chapter Fourteen	117
Chapter Fifteen	125
Chapter Sixteen	135
Chapter Seventeen	145
Chapter Eighteen	153
Chapter Nineteen	161
Chapter Twenty	167
Chapter Twenty-One	175
Chapter Twenty-Two	183
Chapter Twenty – Three	191
Epilogue	199

Chapter One

Welcome to my personal rendition of Ripley's Believe It or Not. I can't believe it, so I'm not sure I can expect anyone else to either. I found myself standing in a cemetery at a funeral for a woman I didn't even know. In fact, until three days ago, I didn't even know she existed. Well, I knew of her because I learned about her in school, but since my eleventh-grade lit class, I hadn't thought about her until my kids, now grown, also had eleventh-grade lit class. I mean, I didn't know, at the time, of any connection I had with her and still don't as I stand here. But I hoped to find out later that day why I was there.

The cemetery was lovely and overlooked the beach. No, not the Gulf of Mexico that's near my Texas home, but the Atlantic, in North Carolina specifically. The cemetery was a lush green carpet of grass and flowers, and I wondered how it could be so green near the ocean, not burned yellow and brown like the cemetery in my hometown in Texas. I surmised that the people in town kept it nice in remembrance of the departed. The trees were large and old, some dripping with Spanish moss, their green branches stretched over the headstones like protective hands. The graves weren't marked with crosses or crucifixes but with chiseled granite and marble stones. They were gray, and ranged from small to large, from simple to ornate. The cemetery reeked of families with money.

The sound of the waves and boats in the distance carried on the wind and relaxed me like a lullaby. The breeze was soft and combed through my hair like a lover's touch. The entire place was beautiful and serene. But even so, it wasn't enough to distract me from the bizarre situation that I found myself in.

Let me explain. A month before, the man-child I'd married and raised, along with our two offspring, for the last twenty-eight years had served me with divorce papers. That's a whole other story I'll save because there is already a lot to unfold here - in this new place. And for the first time since it happened, I can say that it is in the past.

Then a week ago, I was let go from the job I've worked at for seventeen years. The only job for me in my tiny Texas town since the newspaper shut down. With no way to afford the family home, especially with no job and an uncertain financial future while our savings and retirement were in the process of being split and shared, I'm staring down the barrel of nowhere to go and in a hurry to get there.

And then I received this random phone call. A woman professing to be the attorney for Nellie Fontaine, yes, that Nellie Fontaine, tells me that the old woman, who won the Pulitzer Prize for literature, has passed at the age of 102, bless her heart, may she rest in peace. I expressed my sympathies the way any good Southern lady would do and politely inquired as to what that had to do with me. That's when I learned that I, Phoebe Ellis, was named in her will. The attorney further explained that the funeral was in two days and that if I would agree to come, she would forward me a plane ticket.

I am not an idiot. I know all about those rich uncles in Nigeria. But I've never heard of a scam about a retired author from North Carolina. I decided that I needed a vacation just bad enough that I'd risk driving two hours to the nearest airport to see if the boarding pass I was sent worked. I mean, honestly, what in the world did I have to lose?

Surprise, no surprise, I couldn't even figure out how I felt about the whole situation, but that's how I ended up driving a Mustang convertible rental car, also provided by the attorney, Samantha Taylor, to that lovely and obviously ritzy ocean-side cemetery and watched a funeral where I tried desperately to feel something. Anything. But all I accomplished was confusion and disbelief. The only logic I could come up with was that I'd been misidentified, and I hoped like all get-out that I wouldn't have to pay them back for my little mini-vacation. I was sure they would figure out their mistake in no time, but it wasn't my mistake!

I snapped back to attention when I heard the low hum of them lowering that solid mahogany casket covered in a blanket of fragrant spring blooms into the ground. And I joined in the program as each attendee walked to that gaping hole in the ground and tossed more flowers upon the casket. Heavens to Betsy, we are from the South, and we will not let our loved ones suffer the indignity of arriving at the pearly gates without a wealth of leaves and flower petals.

Having dropped their donations to Miss Nellie's afterlife in the grave, most people made their way back to the long line of cars parked in the near distance. A few people stopped to talk to one stoic woman. I was struck by the class that oozed from her every pore. She wore a black pantsuit and white blouse with sensible pumps. From my research on the plane, I assumed she was Miss Nellie's granddaughter, Georgia. Standing beside her was a woman I recognized from her website. Samantha Taylor, Attorney at Law, the attorney who invited me to this shindig. She was also in a suit, but with a skirt, and stiletto heels. I knew I needed to approach them, but I hoped to wait until everyone else left.

I admit I felt like a country bumpkin compared to them. My black Sunday dress and flats felt cooler and more comfortable than their crisp layered attire probably was, but somehow more homely too. Get ready, ladies, I said to myself, here comes the poor relation. Or the misidentified woman you will be so relieved isn't really related to you.

I didn't know what was wrong with me lately. I'm not usually that self-conscious, self-deprecating, or intimidated. But at that moment, I was all those things and more.

When the last person was leaving, the two remaining women noticed me. Samantha made a beeline for me as I wished I could run away. It seemed as though my practical flats had grown roots in the obviously fertile soil and wouldn't budge. Georgia walked away toward a set of benches at the edge of the cemetery overlooking the water.

"Hello, I'm Samantha. Are you Phoebe?" the woman said to me. I assessed she was probably about ten years younger than me.

"Yes, I am. I appreciate you bringing me here. But I think there's been a mistake. I don't know this lady. Sure, I know about her, but why would she name me in her will? Even if she did, I would assume whatever she left for me isn't worth enough to pay for me to fly out here and a premium rental car. It's not like she didn't have any family. I read about Georgia on the internet."

"I'm happy to explain it all to you. Would you like to join us for a chat?" she asked, motioning to the benches where Georgia was now resting. "Do you have time?"

"I have nowhere to be," I said while thinking that, literally, I had no place to be. Over the last week, I had turned the house over to my soon to be ex and loaded all of my personal belongings into a tiny rent-by-the-month storage unit until a judge could help us decide how to split up almost three decades of collected household items and memories.

The lawyer and I walked in silence until we reached the benches.

"Georgia, this is Phoebe," Samantha said. The classy lady a half generation older than me stood up and offered her hand.

"I'm so sorry for your loss," I said, not sure what more to say in this curious situation.

"Thank you, and thank you for coming. I'm sure this seems odd," she said. I loved her accent, clearly well educated, but Southern and different than the Texas one. She spoke slower, and I found her voice pleasant, calming, and comforting.

I laughed despite myself and was immediately embarrassed. "Odd is one word for it," I said. "I'm sorry, I'm just so confused."

"That's understandable," Samantha said. "Have a seat and I'll explain it to you."

I sat, my knees together and ankles crossed the way we have been taught to sit since we were knee high to crickets. I checked my posture was straight, and my hands were crossed on my lap. I was ready for whatever she was about to say. Everything except what came next.

Chapter Two

"Phoebe, thank you for coming. I can't imagine what must be going through your mind or how I would feel and react in your place," Georgia said.

"Thank you. Bizarre is the word that comes to mind," I said. "Then I think it must be a mistake. I also can't imagine how it must feel for you. To have to meet a stranger at this emotional time has to be hard."

"I'll admit that none of this has been easy. Samantha, tell Phoebe what you told me. Maybe hearing it a second time will help me process it all and help it make more sense to me," Georgia said.

"Georgia invited us back to her house for the reading of the will with the other beneficiaries, but it's quite a distance away, so between going to my office here in town or to Hadley Manor, we selected Hadley Manor, so I'll get into those details later," Samantha told me. "For now, I'll explain why you are here as well as what happened in the last days of Nellie's life.

First, let me ask if you are aware of any particular unusual family heritage or history? Any unique gifts or talents?"

"I can't think of anything off the top of my head, but I must say, that's a rather peculiar way to kick off this conversation," I responded, feeling thoroughly bewildered.

"Okay, I shall start at the beginning. This is going to sound surreal, but I assure you it is true. Are you ready?" she asked.

Why did I suspect I was about to be told I was one of those milk carton kids or something, I wondered. "Yes, please explain," I said and couldn't believe how calm I sounded, at the same time wiping the sweat from my hands on my dress skirt.

"You and Georgia and I are distant relatives. Our great-grandmothers were sisters," Samantha explained.

"Get out!" I blurted and then shut my mouth tight. My mouth was betraying my upbringing and making me sound like the country bumpkin poor relation I was feeling like. "I'm sorry." I sighed heavily. "I promise I'm not usually this rude. Please proceed."

"It's okay," Georgia said with a kindness and grace I aspire to one day.

"It's a lot, and there's more," Samantha said. "The three sisters were known as the —" She paused. "I'm sorry. I'm just blurting all this out. It's just that time is of the essence. I wish there was an easier way to say this."

"Go ahead. My imagination is running away with me," I said. "Spies, ladies of the night, moonshiners, serial killers?" I listed, suddenly feeling like I could handle this news. Maybe they were even more questionable than me. Maybe there was a genetic reason for my rebelliousness.

"Witches." Samantha said. Just like that. One word. Seven letters. I sat staring at this woman who looked perfectly normal. I turned and looked at Georgia. Yep, both normal, well-bred, obviously educated women. Wait, me too, I reminded myself. I was also well-bred and educated, no matter how much my self-confidence and financial situation were shaken at the moment.

Samantha continued, "They were known as the Hadley witches. They were the most powerful witches of their time because they were three sisters all born in a year ending in 3."

"Wait, how can we not know this?" I asked. I was always the one with a million questions. And I had at least a million and two at that moment. I reminded myself to stay on track and ask only one at a time. I sometimes came across, to people who weren't used to me, as a lot, too much. And I didn't want to start this new relationship that way.

"In 1931, the sisters were enjoying lemonade on the porch of the family home with some of their children playing in the yard. Nellie was one of those children. A witch hunter came calling and poisoned the sisters. After the funeral, the fathers of those children all went their separate ways and vowed to never connect again nor to talk of their wives' special abilities. They did this in order to protect future generations. That's why we didn't know," Samantha said.

"I'm working hard at not being angry with my grandmother," Georgia said. "I might have accidentally stumbled upon my gifts when I went to Peru to learn shamanism. But when I mentioned that to Grand, she went ballistic, told me I was being foolish, and that I wouldn't inherit a thing if I continued the silliness. I was rebellious and refused to give it up. I even opened a new age book and tools shop. Why didn't she tell me then?"

"I don't know the answer to that," Samantha said. "But I do know that she was sorry for her reaction and her threat."

"So, you two know each other?" I asked. "I'm the only foreigner here?"

"Not exactly. Samantha and I met officially after Nellie died," Georgia said.

"I met Nellie the day before she died," Samantha said. "Nellie decided that she needed to tell Georgia the truth before she ran out of time. But Georgia doesn't have any more family. Nellie wanted to see if there were descendants who could help Georgia learn and cope with this new knowledge. In the process of locating you and me, the woman, a librarian, who helped her was murdered, and as of now, Nellie has been framed for that murder. She was arrested the day I met her. I represented her, got her released on house arrest, and she shared the story with me as well as writing a new will."

"So, you two didn't know you were witches either? What does that mean, exactly? Does anyone know? You look so normal. I look even more mundane, like a suburban soccer mom. Can anyone help us figure this out?"

"I knew that I was a witch," Samantha said. "And I've been dabbling in it a little. My mom is a huge genealogy buff, and she learned about the Hadley witches, and later that we are related to the famous Nellie Fontaine, who was also a witch. But we had not met until Nellie showed up at my office a few days ago."

"Well, at least that explains why I'm here," I said. I stared out at the ocean. As I listened to those waves, I wondered if this was why I never felt like I fit in. At least not since my dad died when I was fifteen years old. "Wait. Hold on a minute. Do you know if it was my mom or dad that was the Hadley? Was he a witch? Because that would explain so much." I hoped someone knew the answer.

"To be honest," Samantha said, "I don't know. But my mom can tell us. We can call her after the reading of the will if you like."

"Thank you. That's very kind of you, and her," I said.

"Should we go to the island?" Georgia asked. "Nancy and Cindy will be arriving soon."

"Nancy and Cindy?" I asked.

"They were my grandmother's housekeepers and companions during the last years of her life," Georgia explained. "Samantha told me they are also named in the will, so I invited them to come for the reading."

"I see," I said. I stood up and felt everything spin just a little. I realized it was like I had been plopped into the middle of some fantasy book. I wanted to ask if there was some magic academy for old lady witches no one knew about, but thank heavens I caught that little bit of snark before it escaped my lips.

"Phoebe, I would say welcome to the family," Georgia said. "But that isn't right. You aren't new to the family. We are just new to each other. I'm pleased to meet you both," she added, reaching out for each of our hands. "Let's go do this."

"Follow us," Samantha said. "I won't lose you; I promise."

We walked back to our cars. Georgia had sent the funeral home limousine away and was riding with Samantha in her Miata convertible. I looked at the two women and something bubbled up inside me. I looked at Samantha's long red hair and Georgia's long blond hair and realized, with my long brown hair, we were the trifecta of hair colors. I remembered that image from social media with three girls sitting together with their back to the viewer with the three colors of hair. I wondered if we all were sporting our natural colors. And then my mouth defied me again.

"How formal is this gathering? What I mean is, you two look so professional and I feel like I'm wearing Sunday go-to-meeting clothes. But I'm feeling that sun, the ocean breeze, and I'm looking at two convertibles sitting here. Do we dare?"

"Darling, you don't need to feel inadequate around us!" Samantha said. "The very fact that you would ask that question can mean only one thing."

"I think we are going to be more than distant relations," Georgia said.

We looked at one another and all said at the same time, "Let's do it!"

CHAPTER THREE

I followed the blue sports car through town and across a long bridge. As soon as we reached the island, there was a gate and a guard house. Not a shack, a real brick building. I hoped that our delay at the cemetery would have sent any well-meaning visitors away, that there wouldn't be the traditional gathering of all the people. The fact that there were guards made me feel secure there wouldn't be a gathering. My eyes widened when I entered the island. It was beautiful with a path lined with flower beds with all types of plants, and my eyes got even wider as my mouth dropped open when I saw the house.

The beachfront mansion appeared to be old but well maintained. Then again, maybe it was the salty ocean air and wind that gave it a weathered look. It was white brick with a wide wraparound porch and balconies on the upper floors and a circular driveway in front. Standing amid the colorful flower beds and manicured lawns, you could see why this beachfront mansion was Nellie's haven. Its wide wraparound porch was lined with rocking chairs and swings that beckoned visitors to enjoy an evening watching sunsets from its vantage point. The ocean was on one side and the intercoastal waterway on the other. The balconies on each floor were furnished with cafe tables and chairs, as well as rocking chairs. It was built of brick, bleached gray from years in the sun and salty air.

There was a car parked in front of Hadley Manor. Samantha pulled into the circle driveway and parked, and I did the same. I was not in the mood to visit with even more strangers, but I didn't want to seem rude or inhospitable either. After all, I was a stranger here too. I secretly hoped the car held one of the housekeepers who was supposed to be here. I'll never understand why people think that when you've said your last goodbye and seen the person who owns a part of your heart lowered into the ground, that you are now ready for a social gathering. But that's how we do things in the South.

I watched as Georgia walked to the sedan while an aged gentleman unfolded himself out of the driver's seat, and I recognized him. Samantha and I followed Georgia.

"Georgia, I'm so sorry for your loss," the man said folding Georgia in a tight hug.

"Jack, thank you for coming. This is Samantha and Phoebe. Ladies, this is an old friend of Grand's, Jack Poe."

Samantha and I both offered hands, shook his firmly, and said, "It's nice to meet you," when he shook ours in return. Then he turned to Georgia and talked to her like we weren't there. I was so proud of myself for even being able to speak in front of this famous man.

"Look, kid, I write horror, but there is nothing more frightening to me than all the people who show up post-funeral. I figured you would rather not have all those folks that were here. So, I told them you weren't coming to the island, and I sent them on their way.

I have two coolers full of food in the car for you and I'll be on my way too as soon as you let me carry it all in for you."

"Thank you so much and thank you for coming all this way for her service."

"I'll help carry a cooler in, if you go and unlock the door, Georgia," Samantha offered.

"I can carry the other," I said.

"Jack, you don't have to leave," Georgia said. "I haven't seen you in so long. But I've been following you, and I've read all your books. I don't watch the movies. They butcher books like a crazed serial killer."

"Thanks, kid," the author said to Georgia with a chuckle at her serial killer reference. "I really do have to go. I must catch a flight back home soon. But I wanted to be here to say goodbye. Nellie was one of the greats. I mean as a lady. She was a fine writer too, but a real lady, and I'm so grateful for her taking a young kid with a dream under her wing, so to speak. I wouldn't be where I am today without her. I'll miss her. I haven't seen her much over the last few years, but we emailed and sometimes talked on the phone. She was always proud of you, you know."

"Thank you. Thank you for coming, for protecting my house from the gawkers, and for saying that. I'm afraid I let her down recently, so it means a lot. Have a safe trip home." Georgia hugged him.

I couldn't wait to hear the story of how Georgia was so chummy with one of, if not the most famous author of our time.

Samantha and I helped get all the food where it needed to go and made a list of the names attached to the dishes. In the near future, the list would be used to write thank you notes. We made a pot of coffee, some sandwiches and sat down at Nellie's kitchen table.

Following Georgia's lead, we all slung our shoes off in the general direction of the back door and let them lie as they fell. Samantha reached into her Michael Kors handbag, that was almost the size of a traditional briefcase, and pulled out a manila envelope. Scrawled across the front in handwriting that appeared to be from a shaky and weak hand was Georgia's name.

"She asked me to get this to you as soon as possible," Samantha said to Georgia. "She recorded it the day she died. It makes me wonder if somehow, she knew."

Georgia accepted the envelope and gently opened it. I sensed that she knew she would someday want it all intact. Inside was a cell phone.

"Just open the videos," Samantha said. "The last video she made is on there. It's to you. She also recorded her will which I converted to text, but I saved that recording too for you."

Georgia took a deep breath, leaned back in her chair, wiped an errant tear from her cheek and stared at the phone.

"Would you rather be alone?" I asked. "We could give you some privacy," I offered.

"I'm just wondering if I'm ready. Maybe I should wait a day or two," she said.

"It's yours, Georgia," Samantha said. "You can listen to it whenever you like, whenever you're ready, and as often as you like."

"I want to listen, and I want to do it with you both, I think," she said.

She pushed play, and I heard for the first time the voice of Nellie Fontaine. I was amazed how strong her voice was, knowing that not only was she over a hundred years old, but that the recording was made on her last day of life. She didn't sound weak at all.

"My dearest Georgia, you have always been and always will be my sweet, amazing girl. I know somehow it was in some entity's divine plan that you would come into my life and complete it the way you did. It was worth losing my beloved son if that's what had to happen for you to be in my life as much as you have been.

"I have no comprehension why a woman who spends her life stringing together words on paper can be so challenged when saying them aloud. I'm realizing it's been almost twenty long years since I was a complete imbecile with you. Since I have so much trouble communicating verbally, I wrote a letter to you. But these decrepit fingers are failing me, and I wonder if even I can read it. Samantha suggested I create a recording for you.

"For half a century, you have been the sunlight, the moonbeams, and the stars in this old woman's life. You've taught me so much, and I bet you never realized that you were schooling the old crone, even more than I was teaching you. But teaching you has been one of my greatest pleasures.

"I can't believe I was as closed-minded as a teetotaling old biddy when you came to me and told me of your trip to Peru and all you were learning. My defense is that I come from a time when people were outcast, even murdered, as you'll soon learn, for having different beliefs than the mainstream. I never wanted that for you. I was terrified for you, and after you learn the truth about our family, I hope you'll understand why.

"It took me some time to realize that this is a new day and age. People are more tolerant about some things. And even if they aren't, you're a strong, capable woman who should be able to choose whatever she wants in this life. I always told you that you could be anything you set your mind to, and I can't express enough my sorrow at not having supported you completely from the beginning, and especially for letting so much precious time slip away from us.

"I turned to the words. I researched all you told me and more. I spent too much time in my life reading fiction and believing it to only be fantasy. Suddenly one day I realized that imagination stems from what we know. I never stopped to consider how much of the fiction we read to escape might be based in a reality of some sort. It turns out I'm quite enamored with thinking about reincarnation, dimensions, and other life forms. I wish I had more time here to explore with you. I wish I had asked you questions instead of rushing to judgment.

"I am so proud of you. I always have been, but no prouder than I am today that you found your own path and that you've stuck to it, despite my disdain. Having lived through a worse time and seeing what the world is becoming, I pray that you and what I believe will be your tribe - the family members I've found for you - can and will make a difference in this world. It can only get better from my perspective, and I'm honored that my sweet girl is leading the way or helping the pack. I'm sorry we haven't been able to talk more about you specifically, your hopes and dreams for this new path.

"You, my love, are the very definition of a unicorn. You are magical. I can feel it. You are rare and beautiful. I know I said I wouldn't be leaving anything to you when I leave this world, and I sure hope you didn't believe that. You, your love, and your time have always been my most prized possession. I know that for years now, you've thought that when it's my time to go that you will be all alone in this world. I also regret not sharing more with you about our family, but there were what seemed at the time good reasons for that too. But you won't be alone. I've come close to finding some sisters for you. Sisters that you will share a heritage and a legacy with, even though you aren't sisters in the true sense of the word.

"But when I go, I hope you understand why I've done what I have. I hope my gift to you gives you peace, security, and pleasure. I pray it will be a haven for any who need it.

"My love is forever yours,

"In this life and the next."

The recording ended, and we all sat at the table staring at the phone. Tears flowed freely down Georgia's face. I wiped my own away, feeling silly for reacting to someone I didn't even know. I had no right. But from the message, despite the obvious chink, theirs was obviously a loving and mutually adoring relationship. The kind I hadn't had since my dad died. I'd be lying if I said that message didn't bring the grief of his loss back to me. I felt guilty to be making such a poignant moment between a grandmother and granddaughter somehow about me. But it was. A moment passed by, and the doorbell rang.

Samantha glanced at her watch. "That's probably Nancy and Cindy. But I'll get the door if you like just in case it's someone else. I told the guards to allow anyone on the island today in case you wanted to receive those wishing to share condolences with you."

"Thank you," Georgia said, wiping the tears from her eyes. "Phoebe, let's move to the living room. We'll be more comfortable there."

I followed her, and Samantha escorted two women into the living room as well. The living room was a cozy and inviting space, with bookshelves and armchairs made from rich cherry wood and a large plush sofa upholstered in buttercream-colored fabric. A bright Persian rug anchored the room and added splashes of bold color. The walls were painted in a pale shade of yellow that reflected the light and brought warmth to the entire space.

We all introduced ourselves and took seats while Samantha returned to the kitchen for her bag and pulled out another envelope. She returned to the living room and stood before us in front of the fireplace flanked with built-in bookcases on either side, crammed full of books.

I soon learned that my great-aunt was a wealthy woman. She left a quarter million dollars each to her two housekeepers. I began to wonder if the cost of my trip would easily be covered by whatever was left to me, a distant niece she'd never met. Honestly, I still didn't understand why she would leave me anything at all. But I wouldn't have to wait much longer.

I'm sure you're in as much suspense about how this story is going to end as I was, so I'll just tell you.

The woman who penned a great American novel in the early 1960s and won a Pulitzer for it, owned a private island off the coast of North Carolina she called Paisley Island. She built a manor on the island after her father passed away. And she left the island and manor to the three of us. Georgia, Samantha, and I were gifted this place. Georgia was entrusted with her financial estate to develop and maintain the island. Nellie's wish was that we turn it into some type of retreat for authors and she even hoped that we would also become authors. But no matter if we did that or not, the one thing we could not do was sell the island, manor, or any part of it.

We all sat stunned for a time. I could imagine that Georgia was shocked to share this place with strangers. What I learned later was that she was just as shocked as I was that she received anything at all. Apparently, she took her grandmother at her word for the threat to disinherit her. Nancy and Cindy were also flabbergasted.

"Miss Nellie told me she had some plans for after she died and she hoped it would mean we could keep our jobs," Nancy said. "I didn't expect anything at all, but I was grateful for the thought I might be able to keep working on the island. I love this place."

The room fell quiet again. Leave it to me to break that uncomfortable silence with an inane question. Of all the thoughts and questions running through my overstimulated mind, the one my mouth chose to voice was, "Why is it called Paisley Island?"

Samantha gave me a funny look. I assumed it was because I asked such a silly question when there were so many more pertinent ones I could have asked. Turns out, she didn't know the answer either.

"I can answer that," Cindy said. "From an aerial view, the island is shaped like a comma or a paisley design shape. Miss Nellie always said Comma Island was too cheeky a name, even for an author, so she called it Paisley Island."

"Makes perfect sense," I muttered.

Nancy and Cindy announced they would be on their way and said that if we needed their services or anything at all, just to let them know. Samantha told them her office would be in touch with them.

After they left, Samantha shared more with us. Apparently, there was a secret attic in this island home called Hadley Manor. And in that attic was all that we needed to learn to be the most powerful witches of our time. It turns out that Georgia, Samantha, and I were all born in the year of 3, Georgia in 1963, me in 1973, and Samantha in 1983.

Earlier in the day, Georgia said she didn't think she was ready to go to Hadley Manor. But now, she was curious about that attic and its contents, and we were all glad we came. I was curious about the whole thing; the island, Hadley Manor, and the attic. I wondered momentarily if I was stuck in some bizarre dream, but realized that in dreams I never thought I was in a dream.

"Samantha," Georgia asked, "I suppose I need to learn to do this, but would you be a dear and let the guards know we do not wish for any more visitors this evening?"

"You've got it, darlin'" Samantha said.

I watched as Georgia sucked in a deep breath and slowly exhaled it. Her eyes were closed, and she took one more deep breath and slowly let it out before opening them.

Georgia looked at Samantha when she disconnected the call. "Do you know what's in the attic? Have you seen it?" she asked the younger woman.

"She showed me how to get into the attic, and she pointed out where and how different things were stored. It was all designed to not look like a witch's attic in case someone ever stumbled upon it. And she said she hadn't been in there since it was packed up and moved here after her father died. But it didn't look dusty or cobwebby enough to me to have been up there for decades," Samantha said. "She did admit to looking for a few items after visiting the library and the librarian's death, what she called the family recipe book. She said others would call it a grimoire, but her family called them recipes. I'm sure that made more sense back then before witches became more mainstream and sensationalized."

Chapter Four

I had no idea what to expect when Samantha, Georgia, and I stepped into the attic of the house we'd just inherited. Samantha showed us the secret entry to the hidden attic Nellie had shown her just a few days before. In the moments before, I'd been buzzing with excitement, my heart racing in anticipation. But as soon as I stepped into the dusty room, all that electricity was replaced by a deep, muted stillness.

Dust motes filled the air, illuminated by a single window that was caked with a lifetime of dust. It had been so long since anyone had opened the window that the latch was stuck and had to be pried open by Georgia.

Samantha, the youngest of us and the only one who had ever been here before, took the lead. Her eyes wide and curious as she moved among the artifacts of our ancestor witches.

"Look!" she said, her voice full of wonder. "It's like a little museum! When I came in here with Nellie, everything was in brown boxes. She showed me how each box was cryptically marked to look like any other attic." Now, there were shelves lining the walls and items on display. It reminded me of an ancient apothecary from a movie set.

Georgia, the oldest of us, and the one who had literally grown up in this house, was more circumspect. After taking a few steps into the attic, she let out a low whistle.

"Wow," she said, her voice heavy with awe. "This is incredible."

The attic was filled with various relics and artifacts, all of them at least a few generations old. There were old books, some of them crumbling with age, and artifacts like ancient jewelry and trinkets.

But the most striking sight was a large portrait of a woman with dark eyes, surrounded by a halo of dark hair. I couldn't help but feel an affinity for her, though I'd never seen her before.

"Who is she?" I asked, my voice barely above a whisper.

"Our ancestor," Georgia said, her voice full of reverence. "The one we never knew. If I had to guess, that would be Nellie's mother, Clara. One of the original Hadley witches."

Samantha gave a small gasp.

"But look!" She pointed to a corner of the attic, where a man lay sprawled on the floor, a pool of dried blood around him.

My heart sank.

"We should get out of here," Georgia said, her voice sharp. *You think?* I caught that remark before it became audible.

But Samantha kneeled down next to the body, her eyes wide with shock.

"He's the one who framed Nellie for the librarian's murder," she said, her voice shaking. "He's the only one who could have exonerated Nellie for that murder!"

"That's--wait, I know that man," Georgia said in a shaky voice. "That's Gordy, Grand's driver. How did he know about the attic? What happened to him?"

We all shared a heavy silence, each of us contemplating the man's tragic fate. How did he even get here? Why did he come? How were we going to clear the famous author's name? Was he the one who unpacked all the boxes? And most importantly, how guilty were we going to look when the police found the dead body of the man who had implicated Nellie in our attic. An attic that now looked like a witch's lair.

Finally, Samantha stood up, her face grim.

"Let's go," she said. Georgia and I both stood there frozen, staring at the man. Samantha reached out, took each of us by the hands and gently guided us out of the attic.

We left the attic, and the man, behind, his fate still unknown. But as I walked away, just from what I saw in the attic, I knew that I had just stepped into a legacy that was both wondrous and terrifying.

"Um, what do we do now?" I asked. "We can't just leave him in there!"

"Anyone got the number to call Ghostbusters?" Georgia asked. I let out a breath I hadn't realized I was holding and relaxed. If these women could be snarky at a time like this, they were my people.

"I need a moment to think," Samantha said. "If we don't handle this just right, we could all end up behind bars."

"I'd rather be sitting at a bar," I said.

"Sugars," Georgia said, "this is where we find out what we're made of. According to the internet, we are best friends if we work together to bury the body. Lordy, I never in all my days thought I would be sayin' you gotta help me hide a body."

"Who could have killed that man?" I screeched. "And what's to keep them from killing us?"

Outside the attic was Nellie's study and one of two libraries in the house. We collapsed into the butter-soft leather seats of the seating area. I felt like I was sinking and wondered if I was about to be swallowed up in some dark hole.

"Think back, ladies," Samantha said, "Slowly and carefully, envision yourself from the moment you walked into the attic. Did either of you touch anything while we were in there?"

"I opened the window," Georgia said. I thought I almost perceived a shakiness in her voice, but it was a true testament to the lady she was that I wasn't 100% sure about it.

"That's fine," Samantha said. "I mean that's part of the house, the house that, as Nellie told it, you practically grew up in. Of the three of us, it's the most logical that your prints would be on a window. Anyone else? If you've traced your own movements and are satisfied you didn't touch anything, think about all of us. Did you see anyone touch anything?"

"I was reaching out to touch a bottle on a shelf," I said. "But that's when you yelled to look, and I didn't ever connect with it. What do we do now?"

"The way I see it," Samantha said, "we have three options. We can try to drag that man out of the house, we can call the security team to make him disappear, or we call the police."

"He was lying in a pool of blood," Georgia said, "besides the obvious physical difficulty of us moving him down three floors, won't we be scattering evidence as we go?"

"Good point," I said and saw Samantha nod. "What if we threw him out the window and then dragged him off?" I said in admittedly not my finest moment.

"Below that window is a balcony. He wouldn't fall but one floor," Georgia said.

"We can call the security team. They can make him disappear," Samantha said.

"What exactly do you mean by make him disappear?" Georgia asked. "Do you mean they're Mafia enforcers who'll roll him into a carpet, lug him out and drive him off the island? And how do we know we can trust them? How long have they worked for Grand? She never mentioned them to me."

"Um, I hired them on Nellie's last day, the morning after she was arrested. The island was full of reporters," Samantha said. "What I mean is they can do the wiggle your nose, wave your arm, and make things, maybe even dead bodies, disappear. They're a magical security company," she explained. "It's risky.

I am, after all, an officer of the court. But if we call the cops, we're going to look guilty as sin."

Georgia and I were sitting on a sofa, and we stared at Samantha sitting in chair with a coffee table between us. Neither of us moved. Did she just say what we think she said?

"But do they do windows?" I asked.

"If that's a realistic, and I use that word loosely, option," Georgia said, "why are we having this discussion? Are we worried about the trust factor?"

I sat in awe, looking at these women, and I wondered if being calm was a symptom of shock and hysteria?

"I'm concerned about the justice factor," Samantha, the attorney, said. "First, shouldn't we try to find out who killed Gordy? Second, Gordy was the man who killed Melanie the librarian. With him dead, and no evidence of that, how do we clear Nellie's name and get justice for Gordy? And lastly, how do we blame a dead guy for a murder, and absolve a dead woman without one of us becoming the next fall guy? And yeah, I don't know how much I trust the security team either, if I'm honest."

"Maybe they killed Gordy." I said.

"If they killed him," Georgia said, "with the ability to zap him away, wouldn't they?"

"Maybe we interrupted them?" I asked.

"I think we should call the police," Samantha said finally. "We did nothing wrong here. We can work together to try to find answers too, but it's the right thing to do."

"You're forgetting one thing," I reminded her. "The body is in a hidden attic, one that looks like a witch museum. Won't the police find that, um, a teeny bit interesting?"

"Probably not as interesting as the BDSM playroom they worked last week?" Samantha said hopefully.

"I've got it!" Georgia said. "What if we just use the security team to move Gordy out of the attic? Could they just zap him to somewhere else in the house? And the bloodstain, could they move that too?"

"Brilliant," I exclaimed. "And, in the process, could they …"

"Find a letter of confession," Samantha added snapping her fingers.

"Boom!" I said, using one of my daughter's favorite expressions she picked up from the students she taught. I wagged my index finger as I enunciated each of the following words. "All wrapped up with a pretty little bow."

Chapter Five

"Are we in agreement?" Samantha asked.

Georgia and I looked at each other, then back to Samantha and nodded. Samantha pulled her phone from a discreet pocket inside her suit jacket and pushed a number.

"Hello, this is Samantha. Who am I speaking with? Hi, Lily. We have a situation at the house and require assistance. Can you send someone? I know this really isn't your purview, but we have something heavy and delicate that we need moved and relocated... Thank you," Samantha disconnected the call and said to us, "She's on the way."

"She?" Georgia asked. "One person?"

"She'll likely call in different people once she assesses the scenario. They all have different skills. She'll decide what's needed and then go from there."

"Why didn't you just tell her?" I asked.

"Because phone calls can be overheard or recorded. They have their own communication methods. We should go downstairs to open the door."

"Why doesn't she just pop in?" Georgia said. Her question sounded sarcastic, not inquisitive. We followed Samantha down the two flights of stairs, and there was a knock before we reached the bottom. I followed Samantha, curious how this was going to play out. But when Georgia reached the bottom of the stairs, she froze and stood staring at the chair lift she'd had installed for Nellie.

"My Grand was the most fiercely independent woman I've ever known," Georgia said. "I worried about her and insisted on her having the lift since she still went to her study on the third floor daily, slept in her bedroom on the second floor, and ate her meals on the first floor, until the day she died."

I was torn between wanting to console Georgia as I watched what looked like a million memories unfolding for her and wanting to hear the conversation between Samantha and Lily.

I hoped Georgia would allow me to share some compassion and empathy with her - later - because the conversation unfolding in the foyer was too intriguing to miss.

"Hi, I'm Lily. What do you need moved?" she asked.

"Come on in and have a seat," Samantha said. "Let me share the situation and then you can call in whoever you think is best. That is, if this is the sort of thing you can help with."

I stood in the foyer, keeping one eye on Georgia and watching Samantha and Lily, the security guard, sit in the library to talk. Georgia was standing on the second step, leaning against the wall and her hand was stroking the arm of the chair lift as though Nellie was sitting there and they were having a loving conversation.

I spent my entire adult life longing for a relationship like that in my life ever since my dad died. He was that person for me. My mom was not a touchy-feely person, my grandparents either. My dad was everything to me, my world, my rock, my cheerleader, my best friend. I lost it all a week before my 16th birthday.

"How can I help?" Lily asked.

"As I said on the phone," Samantha answered, "we need something moved."

"I'm a vampire, with the strength of ten men," Lily explained.

"Okay, here's the situation," Samantha began, "Upstairs, on the third floor, there is a man lying dead in a secret attic."

"I see," Lily said.

"Not yet," Samantha replied. "This man is responsible for the death of a librarian in town. A murder that my late great-aunt is accused of committing because that man told police he drove her there, which is not true. So, these are the things that we need to happen. We need for that man to be anywhere but in that attic before we call the police, and we need for there to be a letter of confession left behind. If you could throw in a reason why he is here that no one knew, that would be great. Because we are also going to have to explain his death."

"I understand the problem," Lily said.

"Good," Samantha said. "Then we can discuss how he is here and who killed him?"

Lily held up her index finger to indicate Samantha should wait. I watched as she pressed her other index finger to her ear as though she was wearing an earbud and began to speak.

"I need Martin, Layla, and Sebastian," she said aloud. I watched as her eyes closed and she stood there silently, with her hand still pressing against her right ear. Her head started to bob from left to right in a move that reminded me of my daughter, Mandy, when she was thirteen. I could never tell for certain if it was a head bob that meant yeah, yeah, Mom, or she had music on in her ears. But this was not a time for our potential savior to be rockin' out.

Lily dropped her hand and looked at me staring at her from the entry hall. I turned to see Georgia standing behind me also watching. Lily waved her hand in a come hither motion.

"Come on in, let me explain how this is going to work. I understand that you, Phoebe and Georgia," she said, wagging that index finger at the two of us, "are new to your magic and this whole world of mystic beings, rules, and so on. Right?"

Georgia and I nodded. Samantha must have told the security team that before we arrived because she never said a word that we heard.

"We understand that Samantha doesn't want the body found in the attic," Lily said. "There would be too many questions, the least of which would be how Gordy got into the house and why he was here, followed by who killed him. My team is on the way. I could move the man, say, from the attic to the study. But that wouldn't move the blood, and it would still mean the cops needing to come to the house, them locking it down as a crime scene, you all being banished from the house and questioned at an uncomfortable police station. So, Sebastian is coming and will be here momentarily to relocate the body and the evidence associated with his death elsewhere on the island. He has the power of telekinesis and can move the evidence better than my sheer strength can."

"What about the evidence that we need to clear Grand?" Georgia asked.

"I see that Samantha envisioned a note left here in the house written by Gordy confessing to the crime," Lily said. "But that won't do. We don't want the police to suspect he was ever in this house, at least not since the last time he drove your relative. Martin will go to Gordy's apartment and leave evidence there. A journal entry about how he was trying to help Nellie by killing the librarian, his confusion about the police saying that he stated he drove her there, and his plan to come here and explain it all to you."

"Brilliant," Samantha said. "But what about him being here on the island, and who but us could have killed him?"

"You instructed us to leave the island open today in case anyone wanted to pay their respects, and we did. We did not keep a log of who was here. The person responsible is supernatural anyway. When the police arrive after we call them because we found the man on our patrol, they will also discover a boat near the lighthouse. They will assume that's how he arrived on the island. Maybe his killer followed him and left."

"Is that what Layla will do? Place the boat and create the suspicions?" Samantha asked, remembering the three that Lily called to assist.

"No. Layla has the gift of manipulating time. Once everything is in place, she will roll back the time to when you arrived directly after the funeral, giving you each an alibi. We will have just called the police about the trespasser discovered on the island.

"Whoa!" I blurted. "This is so surreal. So, just like that we get to do this afternoon over again, and this whole thing just goes away?"

"Not exactly," Samantha said.

"Not by a long shot," Lily said.

"What do you mean?" Georgia asked. "Isn't that the whole problem?"

"Oh!" I said. "No, who killed Gordy and why is still a mystery!"

"And," Lily said as there was a knock on the door, "do they mean harm to the three of you? Are you the real targets?"

CHAPTER SIX

I feel like I need to mention that I have always had the utmost respect for anyone who wears a uniform to work. First responders, military, even back to my childhood days when gas stations had attendants. A uniform usually means you are in service to people. And from my perspective, people are pills most of the time. From hotel housekeeping to hospital employees, they all have my respect. Working with people is hard. Working with people in distress, well, that's just the worst thing, in my opinion. As humans we can be nasty when we are in pain, scared, or stressed. That's my only excuse for what happened next.

We opened the door to Sebastian and Layla. Samantha took Sebastian upstairs to where Gordy was crumpled in the corner of the attic. Layla sat down with Georgia and me in the kitchen and asked us to recall as much as possible about when we arrived at Hadley Manor after the funeral.

We took turns sharing the details of our arriving and Jack being here.

"Wait, Jack Poe? The writer?" Layla asked.

"Yes," Georgia answered. Layla whistled. "He was a friend of my grandmother's."

"What I wouldn't give to meet him. But I don't think we need to go back quite that far. What happened next?"

When we'd shared all the details we remembered, Layla decided the best time to roll back to was just after we kicked off our shoes, when we sat down to eat lunch.

"The way those three pairs of shoes are lying on the floor speaks volumes about three women coming home and getting comfortable, not having just committed a murder," she said.

Georgia and I stared at the shoes. I wondered if I would ever wear mine again. Layla stood up. "You ladies stay here. I'll send Samantha in to see you, and I'll give you a signal. Then take it from the top, or at least from the point that you've put the food away and start making some lunch. Got it?"

Georgia and I nodded. In less than a minute, Samantha came into the kitchen.

"Have they moved him?" Georgia asked. Samantha nodded. "Where did they take him?"

"Sebastian and Lily said it would be best for me to not know," Samantha told us. "Besides, I suspect that when Layla rolls back time, we won't remember anyway."

"I hope not," I said. "I have zero skills in acting, and I'm not the least bit hungry right now. In fact, I might choke if I had to eat a sandwich."

"I'm famished," Georgia said springing out of her chair and going to the fridge. "Can I interest anyone in a sandwich?"

"Yes, I'll help," I said reaching for a loaf of bread we had just set on the cabinet from the collection of food Jack gathered from well-wishers for us.

"Lemonade or iced tea?" Samantha asked, reaching for glasses from a cabinet.

Before we could answer, there was a knock on the door.

"Oh, for crying out loud," Georgia said. "Why can't people leave us alone to grieve?"

"It's not the Southern way," I said.

"Maybe Nancy and Cindy arrived early for the reading of the will?" Samantha said. "I'll answer the door."

It wasn't the housekeepers. It was three police officers from the Lansbury police department. Samantha invited them in and led them to the kitchen.

Georgia froze when she saw them.

"Hello," I said wondering why they were there.

"Georgia, darlin', I think we should sit down. Something's happened," Samantha said calmly.

We walked away from the kitchen bar where we were preparing sandwiches. A variety of meats, cheeses, and vegetables were laid out and ready. There was a platter of deviled eggs and a plastic refrigerator dish of potato salad that we walked away from. I was dying for a deviled egg, but the expression on Samantha's face told me I would have to wait.

We sat at the table and a female officer spoke. She informed us that while the security company was patrolling the island, they discovered the body of Nellie's driver. They wanted to question each of us, especially since that man was the one who provided a statement to the police that he drove Nellie to the librarian's apartment the afternoon that she died.

I was looking forward to telling someone, anyone, the story of how I landed here, that I knew nothing about Nellie or her driver and therefore couldn't be involved. I felt badly for Georgia having to go through this on the day she buried her grandmother. It seemed like they'd been close.

Georgia stayed in the kitchen with one officer, Samantha went to the library with another, and I followed the third to the living room. I was grateful for the opportunity to explain my innocence. The officer listened intently as I recounted my last two days. Any further back than that might give them reason to suspect I had a motive of some kind. She then asked some follow-up questions, but she seemed satisfied with my answers. I hoped it was going as well for Georgia and Samantha. The officer left me sitting in the living room while she went to check on the others. I looked around at the room that I would have sworn I'd never been in before and yet somehow it looked familiar.

Georgia and Samantha joined me, and we all leaned forward in our seats in anticipation of what the officer who seemed in charge was about to say next when suddenly there was a loud crash outside followed by a voice shouting, "Help! Someone help!"

We looked at each other in confusion for a split second before we stood and rushed towards the door to investigate what was happening outside the manor. As we stepped out onto the porch, we saw a woman running across the lawn towards us. She was screaming for help and her face was streaked with tears.

The police officer quickly ran to her side and began asking questions. It turned out that she had arrived on the island by boat with Gordy, Nellie's former driver. He told her they were coming to pay their respects to his former employer.

"I could see the house in the distance, but Gordie said he forgot something on the boat and for me to wait there for him to return. Then I saw security and I hid. I mean I don't know anyone here, but Gordy told me his boss was famous. He never came back. I just saw them taking a body away. I don't know how to drive a boat and I just want to go home!" the frantic woman said.

The police questioned her more about her name, which we learned was Marie, and that this was her first date with Gordy. Poor girl. I'd had some bad first dates in my life, but this was enough to solidify the notion that I didn't really ever want to date again.

I looked at Samantha and Georgia. They were staring at Marie curiously, as though they recognized something about her. Samantha insisted that we would help Marie get home, and the rattled woman agreed.

"Thank you for that," she said. "If I arrive home in a cop car, my landlady will have a herd of cows, and I'll be out on my ear."

We invited her to stay for lunch, and she seemed grateful, so the officers left. We told her to follow us to the kitchen, and she did. But when I turned around, Marie wasn't behind us. It was Lily. And all the memories from earlier, finding the man in the attic, Lily and Sebastian coming to help, all were as clear as could be.

"Wait," I said. "You're Marie?"

"Yes, I thought you needed a distraction, and I gave them more to look for outside the house," Lily explained.

"That's one doozy of a parlor trick, no pun intended," I said. "It's like I remembered none of the afternoon while they were here, and now I recall everything clearly."

"It was better that way. You didn't have to think about the answers to the officer's questions," Lily said.

"You aren't really a security team, are you?" I asked.

"Yes, ma'am. We are Spellman Sentinel Security," she said.

"Nope. You're fixers!" I declared. "Like Olivia Pope. Mystical Magical Menders is what you are!" I said proud of myself.

"I'll tell the boss you said we should change our name," Lily said with a smirk and sarcastic tone. I got her meaning.

"I suppose that would give it all away, huh?" I said deflated.

"Well, you can think of us that way," Lily said kindly, "just don't say it out loud." She chuckled.

"Shouldn't Nancy and Cindy be arriving any minute?" Georgia asked.

"No, the officers are gone, and Layla has turned the time back to where it should be."

"Um, there's just one thing," I said, glancing at the abandoned lunch on the counter. They all looked at me expectantly. "Can anyone tell me, with all this backward and forward time stuff, how long the eggs and potato salad have really been out of the fridge?"

CHAPTER SEVEN

Once everyone was gone and the three of us were alone again, we realized we were hungry and exhausted. I looked at my watch and couldn't believe how late it was. We decided not to take a chance on the food sitting out on the counter, despite what Lily told us about it being fine. It didn't feel cool, more room temperature, and I'm pathologically terrified of mayo food poisoning. I bagged up the food that was out and took it to a trash can outside the back door while Georgia pulled a casserole from the fridge and slid it in the oven.

Standing over that garbage can, I suddenly felt grief wash over me. Georgia was grieving the loss of her dearest and – as far as she knew - last living relative, Samantha was grieving the loss of a new friend. Me? I was grieving the loss of deviled eggs. Please don't judge me, at least I was finally feeling something other than bewilderment. I returned to the house feeling blessed and cheated at the same time. Blessed that I was capable of feeling and cheated from the unrequited hunger for an egg.

Georgia took a deep breath and looked at me for a moment. I could tell something was on her mind. I steeled myself for whatever was about to come next.

"What is it?" I asked.

"Well, I was just wondering, I hate to ask, but I noticed that only three of the rooms upstairs are made up," Georgia said.

Samantha weighed in, "Yes, Nancy made up two of the guest rooms the night Nellie was arrested, and we stayed here with her because it was late."

"Okay," I said, not seeing a problem. There were three rooms made up; there were three of us.

"The problem is, one of those rooms is Nellie's room," Georgia said. "I don't think I can sleep in there. Not yet anyway. I wondered if it would bother you. I was thinking you never really met her, and maybe it would be the same as any other room in the house to you."

There it was. I didn't want to feel that way. And I don't usually take things personally. But how could I not? I was an outsider. The one who didn't even know the rich aunt. The one no one thought should be there.

Now, to be fair, that's not what Georgia said, and no one had actually done or said anything to make me feel that way. But emotions are not rational. So, they wanted to stick me in the dead aunt's room. She was right. I didn't know her. Why should it matter to me?

"Of course," I heard myself say, "that's no problem at all. Or if you would rather no one sleep in your grandmother's room, I am more than capable and willing to make up another room or sleep on a sofa."

"No," Georgia said. "None of us needs to do another thing today."

"I agree," Samantha said. She was pulling a salad out of the refrigerator to go with our casserole. "We don't need to do anything else today. Phoebe, if you aren't comfortable sleeping in there, I don't mind. But I do think we need to make some plans for the next few days while we sort out what we all want to do here."

"I assume you both have lives," Georgia said. "But it would be really nice if we could spend some time together and get to know each other. Is there any chance you could take some time off? We could look at the island, brainstorm how to make Grand's dream come true, and what Hadley Manor is going to mean to all of us."

"Ooh, I love a good brainstorming session," I said, twirling my hair. "But just so you know, my best ideas usually come after a glass or two of wine. Do we have any of that here? And are we really magical? Or is being a witch more like a religion?"

"Both," Samantha and Georgia said at the same time.

"Wow, we really are magical," I said, wiggling my fingers in the air. "I mean, who needs Hogwarts when you have this island?"

Samantha and Georgia exchanged a knowing look, and I suddenly felt like I had missed something.

Samantha looked at Georgia surprised. "You knew?" she asked the older woman. "Nellie suspected that you might but wasn't sure."

"No. I didn't know that I'm a witch," Georgia said. "But as you know, I own the Mystic Moon bookstore, and I associate with all types of people. My best friend is a witch and, ironically, an author. Her name is Micki Borden."

"Oh, so we're not the only ones? That's a relief," I said, feeling like I had just dodged a bullet. "Please tell me she's not a descendant of Lizzie."

Georgia looked shocked. I was instantly remorseful for my words, realizing too late she had just said the woman was her best friend.

"I never thought of that," Georgia said. "I'll be sure to ask her. I was thinking about inviting her to come here too. She could be very instrumental in helping us learn about our gifts as well as how the author community might respond to a retreat here. That is if neither of you have objections."

"I don't," Samantha said pulling the casserole from the oven.

"I only have one reservation," I said. I was impressed with how quickly Georgia was embracing the three of us in this place and not that we were guests. Or maybe she felt that, as guests, we should still be consulted. I wasn't sure. "Please don't ask her about Lizzie. I swear, I am not usually this uncouth, spastic woman that blurts out every thought in her head. I don't know what's wrong with me."

"Really?" Georgia asked. "You don't know? In two days' time, we've totally goobered up your life. Not only revealing that you are some creature that you probably thought wasn't even real, but now my grandmother took the liberty to say, hey, move to North Carolina and make my dream come true, without any regard to the life that you already have. And by saying that we can't sell this place, not that I would want to, forever tying the three of us together, whether we like it or not."

"I don't think she meant to do that," Samantha said. "She wanted to provide a family for you. I don't think there was time for her to realize what it would mean to the rest of us. She knew that I'm not married, and I live here anyway. She had found but not been able to contact Phoebe. She didn't know anything about her. But I think she trusted us to be grown, strong women who can figure it out. Phoebe doesn't have to be here if she doesn't want to be."

"One thing I do love is being talked about like I'm not here," I said. "But trust me when I say, I have no reason to return to Texas. We can talk more about that later this week."

We ate dinner, and as we finished up, Georgia announced that she needed to make a trip to Nags Head.

"I'm up for a road trip," I said, stretching my arms. "But do we have to take the broomstick? I'm generally allergic to all cleaning products and implements."

Georgia chuckled. "No broomsticks, we'll take my car."

"Phew, thank goodness," I said, relieved. "I was worried I'd have to brush up on my flying skills. I haven't flown since I was a kid, and I don't want to crash and burn."

I was looking forward to some girl time and getting to know more about these women that Georgia so eloquently pointed out I would be tied to for the rest of my life. But I really wanted to return to the attic too and have a good look at everything there. And there was some research I was dying to do on my computer. There were so many questions.

My intention to do some research after we all went to bed flew out the window as soon as I crawled into bed. I suppose I hadn't realized how much the trip and the hiccup day had taken out of me. I decided I was going to call the day of Nellie's funeral the hiccup day. That's what it felt like to have two different realities for part of the day. I wasn't a fan of this time blipping thing. I recalled books where characters traveled in time. It seemed interesting until it happened to you. Reliving an hour blew my mind, I couldn't imagine traveling years or centuries. It all seemed so absurd.

Anyway, I fell asleep fast, and I slept hard. And I dreamed. As I began to stir awake, I heard a sound and froze, holding my breath so I could listen better. It was the screech of an owl. It sounded close and I smiled.

When the room returned to silence, I realized that for the first time in my life, I woke up remembering my dream and that it had displayed in full color. It was a simple dream, nothing worth commenting on. I was just watching a woman walking on the beach. But I clearly recalled the color of the water, the sand, the beach grass, her dress, and her hair. I wondered if it meant that I would find a home here. Maybe even a life. And did I even dare to possibly imagine a lifelong dream coming true? One I had thought my chance of seizing was long gone?

The drive to Georgia's house was four hours each way. So we had a light breakfast and left early hoping to be back in time for dinner.

"My mom told me something, Phoebe," Samantha said finally, her voice barely above a whisper. "She said it was your father who was the descendant of the Hadley witches."

The news sent a flood of memories through my mind. I remembered my father's stories of the mysterious women appearing on stormy nights, bearing warnings of the dangers of the sea. I recalled the old family bible my parents kept on the mantle, its yellowed pages tucked into the back and the signature of a woman who was not my grandmother scrawled in its margins. I thought of my mother's shuddering silence every time the subject of our family's past came up.

"I guess that explains a lot," I said, and Samantha nodded in agreement.

Georgia shared with us a story about going to Peru where she and her friend spent two weeks with a shaman in the Amazon. During this time, she embraced some powerful beliefs and began to find a quietness about her soul. She learned of the infinite possibilities that were available to all creatures, no matter how small or insignificant they seemed.

Georgia also developed an understanding of how the world worked that was both mysterious and amazing. It was as if she were seeing things differently, as if she were gradually awakening to a new reality.

But in all of this, one thing remained consistent: Georgia never realized that she actually had any magical powers. She just didn't believe it; it seemed too impossible. It wasn't until later, back in the United States, that she began to feel something stirring inside of her — a realization that perhaps there really was more than what was visible to the eye.

It was then that a seed had been planted deep within her, and as time passed, it would slowly start to grow into something truly extraordinary. Georgia believed that some possessed magical powers, but she wasn't one of them.

And then, it happened. Georgia asked about me. She was driving and glanced at me in the backseat in her rearview mirror. These women seemed so accomplished. So put together. And I felt like my whole life had crumbled into a heap of ruins. But I decided that I had to tell them, be honest with them.

"I hope you don't mind if I start with my dad," I said. "That's when my life was normal and wonderful. He and I were two peas in a pod, peas and carrots. I think my mother always resented that. He was my champion, the one who made me believe I could do anything."

"What did you want to be when you grew up, Phoebe?" Samantha asked.

"I always thought I would be a writer. I wanted to write books. Instead, my dad died, I ended up taking care of a super dependent mother, got married right out of college and raised that man along with our two children. And while I'm disclosing, I'll go ahead and tell you that a month ago he asked for a divorce, and last week I lost my job. So, you see, I have no burning reason to return to Texas."

"Oh, I've been there," Georgia said. "The whole emotionally absent mom thing is why Grand and I were so close. My dad died in the Vietnam war when I was three. My mom never got over it."

"I've never been able to focus on men enough," Samantha said. "I've wanted to get married, have a family of my own. But I get so hyper focused on my job, I literally forget about them! Who does that? What woman forgets she has a date or a boyfriend? Just shoop," she said making a motion with her hand over her head, "gone, forgotten. I never intended to be career-focused like most other attorneys. I just am."

"Wow," I admitted. "I was feeling so inadequate compared to you both. I kept thinking at the funeral I was the poor relation. Not only financially. But in everything. We really do have things in common, don't we?"

"That's my Grand," Georgia said. "Even though I sounded angry last night about her making assumptions and decisions for us, I also knew that she had a sixth sense about things like this. And if she thought we could work together, she was probably right."

"Not to boast or anything, but it seems like we cleared her name in one day," Samantha said. "Who knows how much we are going to be able to accomplish together. And Phoebe, I suspect that your dream of becoming a writer is still possible!"

CHAPTER EIGHT

We arrived at Georgia's house in Nags Head. It was a white beach house with a blue roof and shutters, nestled into a sandy dune overlooking the glistening ocean. A wrap-around porch with weathered wooden stairs led up to it. The windows glinted in the sun, and there was a rocking chair on the porch. The windows were decorated with white flower boxes, and the porch was lined with sand-encrusted seashells. There was a briny smell from the sea, mixed with sweet hints of jasmine and gardenias from nearby gardens and blooming flowers.

Inside, she invited us to the kitchen for a glass of lemonade. Her kitchen was everything one would expect for a new age woman who loved luxury. White marble countertops and shiny steel appliances filled the room, along with cabinets in soft pastel shades, giving off a modern air of sophistication. The room was bathed in sunlight streaming through the large windows, highlighting cozy cushioned armchairs by the breakfast nook, and decorative glass dishes placed on open shelves.

"If anyone needs it, the little girl's room is down the hall on the right," Georgia told us. "Make yourselves at home. It won't take me long to pack."

Georgia headed down the hall to gather her things, and when she returned, one piece of her luggage was quivering and gyrating. The growling and hissing emanating from the bag was surprisingly loud, echoing off the walls like a distant thunderstorm. The noise resonated with an unsettlingly intense power, as if something powerful were contained within. Most people would assume there was a small pet in that bag. But I had just learned that I and these other women were witches. I was afraid to assume anything on this weird day.

"Um, Georgia, should your bag be quaking like that?" I asked.

"No, it should not. But that's Venus, and she isn't especially fond of travel."

"Plucking a star wasn't enough for you?" I muttered low. But not low enough.

"Would it be for you?" she asked and smiled at me.

I was delighted that my typical snarkiness was not going to be frowned upon by these ladies, and they were going to be worthy opponents.

"I'm ready," Georgia said. "Thanks for coming with me. I know it's a long trip."

"I'm enjoying seeing the area. It's even more beautiful than I imagined," I said picking up one of Georgia's suitcases but avoiding the one emitting angry growls.

Georgia picked up the cat carrier and said, "Let's go. I thought we could pick up some shrimp tacos for lunch and get back before dinner."

"Georgia," Samantha said. "Could we stop by your bookstore? It's one of my favorite places here. We can still make it back for dinner."

"Oh, yes, please. I would love to see it!" I added.

"Thanks, girls," Georgia said. "I really wanted to go by there too, but I didn't want to take up too much time."

The bookstore was fascinating. An eclectic collection of books, candles, crystals, oracle cards, crystal balls, and cauldrons were on display as well as an assortment of herbs.

We met the co-owner, Max. It turned out he was also Georgia's significant other. I couldn't wait to ask about that once we were on the drive back home.

And now that I knew that Georgia embraced things like witchcraft, I wondered how she never knew she was a witch. I mean, now that I know, I'm thinking back on things that suddenly make more sense or, at the very least, inspire me to ask questions I never thought to ask. I secretly planned to consult the Google search on our way back to Paisley Island while I was in the back seat and hope no one noticed. I don't know why it seemed better to search for information instead of just asking the two women I was with, who seemed to know a lot more about it than I did. But it felt important to verify with an independent source.

But my plan was thwarted again when Samantha insisted on taking a turn in the back seat despite my assurances that I was perfectly comfortable there. I didn't want to appear rude by using my phone where someone could see me, so I waited to return to my room that night.

"So, Georgia," I said, "I didn't realize that your life was so far away. A job with the library, owning a store, and Max. It kind of feels like you are the one giving up the most if we pursue making something permanent from Paisley Island. How do you feel about that?"

"I don't suppose I've had the time to process it all," Georgia answered honestly. "But I didn't sleep well last night and had a lot of time to think about it. I have options. I don't need the library job. It just helped keep me busy, and I reckon I've kept going to work out of habit more than necessity. Max can run the bookstore, or we could move it closer to the island. I haven't decided how I want to approach that."

"How long have you been together with Max?" I asked.

"Ten years," she answered with a nonchalance I found intriguing.

"Ten years?" Samantha asked.

"Yes," Georgia answered with a smile and a chuckle. "He asked me to marry him. Five times, in fact. Every two years he tries again. I love him, but I love my own space even more. I suppose that sounds shallow of me."

"I totally get that!" I said. "One thing I've vowed is to never have to share a bathroom again. But how is that going to work out if you're running a bed and breakfast kind of retreat? Not only would you not have your own space, you would be surrounded by strangers."

"I have some ideas. Want to hear them?" she asked us.

She sounded excited, and we couldn't wait to hear.

"My vision is to convert the old family manor into a bed and breakfast with a variety of rooms in the main building. That way, they can be inspired by the natural beauty and energy of this place while having their own personal space. And we could have a communal area where everyone can gather together in one spot, like an enchanted garden or something."

Georgia seemed so passionate about her ideas that it was hard not to get caught up in her enthusiasm.

She continued talking as though she had been planning this retreat for years. "I'd also like to build some smaller houses on the island for people looking for more permanent residence. That way, it would become a permanent haven for those seeking solace from life's difficulties or maybe just needing some time away from the hustle and bustle of everyday life. But I think we should limit it to authors who believe like we do."

"Do you mean, Baptists need not apply?" I asked, raising an eyebrow.

"Of course not, as long as they're Baptists that believe in magic," Georgia said with a wink.

"I can see the advertisements now," Samantha said, holding up her phone. "New exclusive community! If you're an author with magical gifts and a penchant for seclusion, apply at witchy authors dot com."

"Hmm, I wasn't thinking about advertising," Georgia said, frowning slightly.

"So how would we get the word out about this uniquely niche community?" I asked, tapping my chin.

"I know people," Georgia said, flipping her hair. "I've spent my whole life around authors, as the granddaughter of Nellie Fontaine, a librarian, and a bookstore owner. I've had the opportunity to meet dozens of authors. Some I know have an awakened mind, like my friend Micki. There are others too. And then word of mouth. Anyone we don't know, we will invite for a short retreat until we vet them."

"Because I know so many authors," I said. "How about you, Samantha? Do you know any cool authors with magic powers?"

"So, so many," the attorney said, pulling out her own phone. "Let me just scroll through my contacts... Ah, here's one! Jane Spellman, author of 'The Witch's Guide to Winning Friends and Influencing Spirits.' She's got a wicked sense of humor and a killer wardrobe."

"I'm sold," I said, grinning. "If Jane Spellman is in, then I'm in too. But can we make sure the houses have a Jacuzzi? I can't live without my bubbles."

"Of course, sugar," Georgia said, smiling at me. "We'll make sure you have all the bubbles you need. And maybe even a magic wand to control them."

We all laughed, feeling giddy with excitement about the possibilities of this new venture. Who knew that being named in a random long lost great-aunt's will could lead to something so magical and extraordinary?

When we returned to the island, Georgia drove us around the island and said we could take a walking tour the next day.

"I had no idea the island was this big!" I said.

"It's not far-fetched to think we could build a tiny city here," Samantha said.

"We could have businesses too?" I asked.

"I don't know how many businesses we could support, but if we get creative, we might could find a way."

"So I get that," I said. "And I understand the need and desire for privacy and all, but how much draw do you think we could get if we did one or two open-house-type events a year where visitors could come, buy autographed books, meet the authors, buy souvenirs, make it a festival of some sort?"

"Paisley Palooza?" Samantha proposed.

"Yes!" I said.

"That's a brilliant idea, Phoebe! We can do some market research on that," Georgia said. "If the authors donated their time and books and all of that weekend's proceeds went into a community fund, maybe we could pay for employees for a couple of businesses. We just need to figure out what would be the most important ones."

"Well, apparently, we already have the body removal service on the premise. I wonder what other talents they have?" I snarked and was so relieved when Georgia and Samantha laughed with me.

"Darn, I should have checked to see what's going on in that case," Samantha said. "I got so entranced hanging with you girls today that I forgot all about it."

"Oh, dear, what does that say about us?" Georgia mused. "Poor Gordy, and here we are out on a road trip having a blast."

"Bless his heart," we all exclaimed at the same time.

"I think it says that you, in particular, have your own grief to deal with," I said. "Not to mention, we just learned we're witches and had to deal with finding out vampires and magic are real, compound it with the expectations of Nellie, and we are dealing with a lot! Samantha, tell me if I'm wrong, that us not calling and hounding about the investigation, thus giving the appearance that we are grieving is likely the best thing we could have done. They will never know that we had fun getting to know each other, thinking about our futures, eating delicious shrimp tacos. They won't know, right?" I said hopefully.

"We can always hope," Samantha said.

CHAPTER NINE

I was really new to this idea of spirits from the other side of the veil being able to communicate with those of us on our side. I mean, I'm from Texas. We're acutely aware of things like Dia de Los Muertos - the day of the dead - when the veil is thinnest between the two worlds. I knew that some people believed they could communicate with their loved ones who had passed on. But as we sat in Nellie's kitchen eating another warmed casserole, I really hoped she was able to look down on us, and that she found it as fun as we did.

After Georgia shared her vision for what Paisley Island could become, we sat around Nellie's table with a yummy cheese topped concoction and a delightful bottle of wine and played a game. Actually, two games rolled into one (that might have been the wine talking).

If money were no object, what would be the best community we could imagine for authors? Followed by a game also played in the business world, "Yes, and." As a woman who spent decades working in the manufacturing industry, I was no stranger to brainstorming. But I couldn't imagine a time that I had more fun.

"Writing spaces should have a lovely view," Samantha started.

"Yes, and writing spaces should have an abundance of natural light," Georgia said.

"Yes, and writers should be able to control how much light," I said.

"Yes, and authors shouldn't have to clean their own rooms or houses," Samantha said.

"Yes, and regular shopping should be delivered," Georgia said.

"Yes, and there should be an inspiring garden," I added.

"Yes, and coffee. There should always be coffee," Samantha said.

"Yes, and chocolate," Georgia said.

"Yes, and a walking trail," I said.

"Yes, and tables to write seaside," Samantha said.

"Yes, and thick, soft towels," Georgia said.

"Yes, and puppies," I added, missing my tiny teacup Maltese I'd left with my daughter in Texas. I was really missing her.

"Puppies?"

"Oh, absolutely! Think about it, who wouldn't want a cute little puppy to snuggle with while they're struggling with writer's block? Plus, they could act as writing assistants and offer their adorable insights on character development," I said with a grin.

"Uh, I don't think that's a great idea," Georgia replied.

"Well, you can't blame me for trying. After all, if money were truly no object, we could hire a whole team of writing puppies to inspire us!" I retorted, winking mischievously.

Georgia chuckled, "Okay, okay, you got me there. But in all seriousness, this community for authors sounds like a dream come true. Now, let's keep brainstorming!"

We got down to the nitty-gritty and started a list of the tasks involved in making this happen.

"How long do you think it would take to build this?" I asked.

"In reality, it could take years. But I don't want it to take years. I would love to have this up and inhabited by Halloween," Georgia said. "What's the pagan holiday for Halloween?" I asked Samantha.

"Samhain. It's the witch's new year celebration. It's the culmination of Halloween and Day of the Dead."

"What a lovely tribute to the Hadley witches," I said.

"Um, you mean the original Hadleys or the new Hadleys?" Georgia asked.

"All of us!" Samantha exclaimed. "What a lovely tribute to Nellie."

"Is that even possible?" I asked. I had acquaintances and co-workers who had built houses and it seemed like it always took longer than expected. And that was for a single house. Here we were talking about a dozen houses to be built simultaneously.

"It's probably not the best use of our money," Georgia said, "But if we can hire multiple contractors, it could go faster."

"What if we used contractors with help?" Samantha asked.

"What do mean?" I asked.

"You mean like the security company? Builders with special talents?" Georgia clarified.

"Exactly!" Samantha said.

"Whoa, hold on a minute here," Georgia said. I poured the last of the second bottle of wine into our glasses. "One thing I insist upon is quality. This house was built 70 years ago, and it's still standing, none the worse for wear. It's withstood countless hurricanes. I don't imagine a house that someone waves a wand to create would be as durable."

"Maybe not," Samantha admitted. "But that doesn't mean that some things can't be done more efficiently. We wouldn't take shortcuts like making concrete dry too fast, but if workers had extra speed, for example, when it comes to hammering nails, it would mean fewer workers needed for each house."

"That makes sense to me," I said. "But are there seriously companies like that? That use magic to do their work? Is there a special witches and werewolves phone book? How do you find them?"

"Word of mouth!" Samantha said. "Vampires and werewolves need jobs too. I found the security company because of one of my legal clients. But I bet the security team might know of some mystical sorts who construct houses, do landscaping, and so on."

"What about gnomes that make the gardens cute in the daytime, but sneak into our houses at night and clean them while we're sleeping?" I asked. They both laughed. I guess they thought I was teasing.

"You said our houses," Georgia said. "Does that mean you plan to stay here?"

"If there's room for me. If I can be useful. Why not? But I'm not an author, and this is a community for them."

"Phoebe," Samantha said, "Nellie said she hoped we would all give writing a try. But of the three of us, you are the one who is already a writer. Why wouldn't this be a place for you?"

"I write technical manuals," I said shaking my head. Without even realizing it, my frustration of being trapped in that unimaginative job came through in my voice. "I hardly think that's what Nellie had in mind. I always wanted to be an author, but I'm fifty years old and I don't have the first clue how to go about writing a book!"

"I know someone who can help!" Georgia said. "My good friend Micki Borden! She can help us learn the steps to writing good books, and what would help make this an amazing community for authors. She'll be here tomorrow, and I can't wait for you to meet her.

But before I knew it, we were off on another brainstorming session where magic could make life wonderful. It was all fanciful of course. Wasn't it?

I slept deeply that night. But I dreamed again of the woman walking on the beach, but this time in more detail. The woman was blond and petite. She was wearing a tasteful navy dress with white trim reminiscent of a sailor's outfit, like something from the '80s. Her feet were bare, and she carried a pair of sandals in her hand. Her fingernails and toenails were polished in matching bright pink. She had long layered hair with curls, also from the same decade, a Farrah Fawcett *Charlie's Angels* style. She walked along the beach, and I thought it looked similar to the beach at Paisley Island, though not identical.

There was a house at the woman's back. A sprawling three-story estate with a true wraparound porch around all four sides and balconies on each floor on every side of the house. I recognized it immediately as Hadley Manor. The woman was walking away from the house.

The dream felt like I was walking along behind the woman, who looked back over her shoulder as though she felt someone watching her. But she seemed to stare right through me. She didn't see me. It was nearing sunset, but there was still enough light to see dark clouds forming along the horizon. The wind was brisk off the water. The woman turned right, walking away from the surf and into thick foliage.

I began to walk faster, trying to catch up and not lose sight of the woman. But when I reached the high grasses, the woman was nowhere to be seen. I walked slowly into the grasses, watching for where they were bent or looked trampled and followed the path for what seemed like a mile until I found myself on the bank of a small lake. I still couldn't see the woman anywhere, but there was a large boulder, and I decided to take a seat and rest a moment, before walking back to the house. It was now dark, but the full moon lit the lake enough to see the edges around the black water. I leaned against the largest rock, which looked as though it had been strategically placed next to two substantial but smaller rocks.

Lightning struck, and with the additional light something caught my attention. Flapping in the breeze was a small piece of fabric, caught under the edge of the stone, and I reached down and picked it up. It was a piece of weathered fabric, fragile and bleached by the sun, but it was outlined with cording. I realized it was a piece of the woman's dress. It looked old, aged by the elements. I looked around perplexed and felt like somehow a lot of time had passed since our walk from the beach. Time as in years or decades.

I awoke to the sound of the owl again, and I walked to the French door that led to a balcony and pulled back the curtain to peer out and see if I could see it. It was just before sunrise with a cloudless sky and bright moon. I couldn't see the owl. I opened the door to see if it screeched again and I could tell what direction it was coming from. No sooner had I opened the window, the bird landed on the balcony railing.

I thought I was awake, but apparently, I was still dreaming.

"Thank goodness you've arrived," the owl said.

I stared at the bird in wonder. Its voice was deep and resonant and a little bit gravelly.

"Um, what?" I asked, sure I was hallucinating.

"I've been waiting for you forever," it said.

"How did you know I would be here?" I asked, perplexed.

The owl rolled his big, expressive eyes. "Well, I am your familiar, dear. It's my job to know where you are and what you're up to. And believe me, I've been keeping an eye on you for quite some time."

I couldn't help but laugh at the absurdity of the situation. "You're my familiar? Like from Harry Potter?"

The owl let out a long-suffering sigh. "No, not like from Harry Potter. I'm a real owl, thank you very much. And I take my duties very seriously. You're lucky to have me, if I do say so myself."

I couldn't help but feel a little bit giddy at the idea of having my very own talking owl as a familiar. "So what do we do now?"

The owl hopped off the windowsill and spread his wings, looking very dignified. "Now we get to work. You have a lot to learn, my dear. But don't worry I'll be here to guide you every step of the way."

I grinned, feeling a sense of excitement and adventure bubbling up inside me. "Alright, let's do this. Wait, is this real?"

"Oh, you silly girl!" the owl said, "You're awake! This is no dream. I'm a messenger of sorts. To help you heal and start your journey."

"My journey?" I asked.

"To begin your life as a writer," he said. "The two are intertwined you know." he said.

No. I didn't know, but I sensed that something was about to happen.

Chapter Ten

The bird flew away and I stood there watching it. It was a beautiful bird, a barn owl with varying shades of brown on its back and wings. Its chest and underneath the wings was white. He wasn't a huge bird, but I thought, what a strange but wonderful familiar. I always thought of a familiar as something that lived in the house with you, not a wild animal. I called out into the trees, "But how will you know when I need you?"

I heard a swoosh, and the owl landed on the balcony.

"Oh," I said startled. "You heard me!"

"Yes, ma'am. I have very good hearing, but here's something you should know about me. As your familiar, we can communicate telepathically as long as we are within 100 feet of each other. I will rarely stray farther than that. But if you go on a long trip in a vehicle, like yesterday, I will have a harder time following. My maximum flight speed is twenty miles per hour. If you're walking, I'll be there for you; in a car for a short distance, I'll catch up; but hauling whiskers along an interstate, I'm doomed."

"I see," I said. "So - you can hear my thoughts?"

"Indeed, I can. And I'm pleased you feel I'll be a wonderful familiar. I'm not strange, though. I think you're going to find some much stranger familiars in the very near future. It's time for me to nap, and you have incoming to get ready to meet," the owl said.

"Wait, one more thing," I said.

"Try communicating with me without words. That's going to be important sooner than you think," the owl instructed.

I closed my eyes tight and tried to push my thought toward the owl until I realized I probably looked like a toddler trying to take its first conscious dump, and I burst out laughing.

I then heard the owl in my head. I was looking right at it, and the beak wasn't moving. But I heard clearly, "My name is Sage, but if you prefer to call me something else, I'm amenable. I prefer to live outside, but if you feel safer, we can negotiate some inside living arrangements."

That was exactly what I was wondering. But Sage had more to add.

"I prefer to hunt my own food. It helps protect my girlish figure," Sage said. "Now, hurry along. It's going to be a big day."

I returned to my room and had an odd notion that I wanted to leave the door open. I was reluctant to close Sage out. But it was already a warm and humid morning, so I closed the door and headed for the shower.

For the first time, I started thinking about how living on a private island was so different than the life I had always known. When Nellie lived here, she had the most distinct privacy. She could have had no coverings on the windows. She could have walked the island naked with no one to see. And our plans were going to wipe that away. Yes, we would be picking our neighbors wisely. But the island would never be the same.

Dressed for the day, and not sure what it would bring, I headed down to the kitchen for desperately needed coffee. Georgia was already there.

"Good morning!" I said.

"Good morning. I hope you slept well," Georgia said. I thought she was going to make a fabulous hostess.

"I did," I said. "I sleep really well here. But I have the most vivid dreams. I wanted to talk to you and Samantha about them this morning. Has she come down yet?"

"Yes, and gone. She's gone to get Hazel and check on the investigation into Gordy's death," Georgia said. But I also heard a low growl and noticed a gorgeous cat sitting in Georgia's lap. The black Persian cat had long, silky fur that was a rich, deep black that glimmered in the sunlight pouring in through the kitchen window, while the tips of her fur were tinged with a subtle grey hue and gave her a smoky appearance.

Her thick, luxurious coat cascaded down her body like a velvety waterfall and puffed out around her head in a full, thick mane.

But it was her eyes that truly captivated me. Bright, amber globes peered out from beneath her elegant, curved brows, shining like two orbs of liquid gold. They were warm and expressive, filled with intelligence, curiosity, and a hint of mischief. They seemed to hold a secret, a knowledge beyond the comprehension of mere mortals.

She exuded an air of regality and mystery, her elegant form and piercing gaze commanding attention and respect. She was a creature of grace and beauty, a feline goddess in her own right and deserving of her name. I momentarily forgot about Samantha and my dream.

"Oh, my, is this Venus? I'm pleased to make your acquaintance, Venus. Is my presence distressing you?" I asked.

"No," Georgia said. "It's not you. It's the thought of Hazel." She stroked Venus's back and directed the next words to her, "Now, you stop that. It's going to be fine, and you're going to be a good kitty. It's only for a few days until Samantha returns to her house on the mainland. I expect you to be a nice host, or at least mind your manners."

"Yes, Hazel. Okay," I said. For some reason this tiny black lion had totally discombobulated me. "So Hazel is another cat? A dog? Does Venus not like the idea of another animal, or is it something specific? I assume they've never met since you hadn't met Samantha, right?" I asked while pouring a tall cup of coffee and silently blessing Nellie's heart for having big coffee mugs.

"Right, they've never met. She's not fond of other animals. Typical cat, you know, thinks she the center of the universe. And frankly, she is the center of mine."

I thought about my new pet, napping in a tree nearby, "So what kind of animal is Hazel?" I asked.

"A hedgehog."

"A what did you say?" I asked again. I was sure I didn't hear that correctly.

"A hedgehog named Hazel is what our new friend has as a pet. I suppose for someone who forgets boyfriends, a small animal that lives in an enclosure and won't die if forgotten for a day is the perfect choice. Unless she were to have a cat. A cat would be good. They are fiercely independent, except at mealtime of course."

"Alrighty then," I said. "So Samantha's off to rescue her forgotten pet and returning. What's on the agenda for today?"

"Micki should be arriving," Georgia was saying when she was interrupted by the doorbell. "Remind me to tell the sentinels at the bridge that even if we tell them someone is coming and they should allow them on the island, they should call and let us know that they are here," she said setting Venus on the floor and going to answer the door. Venus looked at me. Her ears perked up, and she darted out of the room.

"Noted," I said.

Georgia opened the door, and I loved eavesdropping on the warm and comfortable greeting of two good friends. Friends who had known each other for a long time. That's something I never managed to have what with taking care of

Mother, the ex, and the kids, and working full time. I knew other mothers and co-workers but not anyone that I ever felt close to, not in the way these women seemed. They rounded the corner into the kitchen, just as the back door opened and Samantha came through carrying a big clear plastic tote.

"Look, the gang's all here!" Georgia said and introduced us all to Micki.

"You look really familiar to me," I said to Micki. "Is it possible I know you from somewhere?"

Georgia and Micki chuckled.

"Now that you mention it," Samantha said, "You look very familiar to me too. How could that be possible unless..."

"Is it okay for me to tell them?" Georgia asked, looking at her friend.

"I will. Hello, ladies, it's so nice to meet you both, and I really look forward to getting to know you. Georgia invited me here to help you with your newfound powers and to help plan the dream island. But in order to do that effectively, I think we have to be open and honest. So my name is Micki Borden, and I've been a practicing witch for about three decades now. But in my professional life, I'm an author who writes paranormal romance novels. And I do so under a pseudonym. You probably both recognize me as Natalie Duceman."

My mouth fell open, I stared at her for only a moment until the room started spinning. The voices around me as Samantha shook hands with the lady sounded like I was underwater, and a black fog was creeping in from all sides. Before I knew it, the world went black and silent.

The next thing I remember was waking up hearing Georgia saying my name over and over. I felt a shake. and I tried to open my eyes. They fluttered a bit involuntarily before I managed to keep them open, and focus came back. I was lying on the kitchen floor. I had just embarrassed myself and passed out in front of my all-time favorite author. My idol. She was here to help me learn to be a witch and, Georgia had said, also to help me become the writer I always wanted to be. I know this sounds weird. But that was even more unbelievable to me than me being a witch, a co-owner of a private island, with a security team of supernatural creatures, and with a talking owl outside my bedroom.

Georgia and Samantha helped me up. I took a deep breath, and I wondered if my life could get any more bizarre?

Chapter Eleven

We all sat down at the kitchen table, and I began to apologize. "I'm sorry. it's just been —"

"A lot," Georgia finished for me.

"I can't imagine," Micki said. "I'm flattered and horrified. I'm sorry. Maybe we should have led with the Natalie Duceman bit.",

"No," I said, "It's not your fault. It's just that mere days ago, I was in Texas, a woman who was put out to pasture not only by her husband and children, but also her job. I remember sitting there, wondering if life was over for me. I felt like I had no worth. That I had given my best years to people who didn't even want me anymore. And then I got this outrageous phone call that I'm the great-niece of a living legend, well, a no longer living legend, and then all of this. Add to all the things you already know, some wildly explicit dreams, and this morning, a talking owl on my balcony. I feel like I need help for sure. But you guys may not be qualified to help me."

"What kind of dreams?" Samantha asked.

"A talking owl?" Micki inquired.

"We're all a little out of sorts, but I know it's going to be okay," Georgia said.

"If I may," Micki said. "First things first. Everyone, take a deep breath. We will unravel and untangle this. I know Samantha has a bit of experience, and I hope I can help with any gaps. What if Samantha and I get some coffee. Georgia, I presume you already have a notepad?"

Georgia nodded.

"Great, then let's brainstorm a list of all the things that we need to sort out and start prioritizing them," Micki said, taking control of the situation like a boss. "Samantha and I can figure out how to help you two the best. We're going to have this all under control in short order. I promise."

"You really must be a wizard," I snarked, not being able to imagine anything being in order anytime soon.

"Look, you three, individually, are forces to be reckoned with. You are the wind, the fire, and the rain, each of you a powerful storm. But together, you are a fierce hurricane. If you are organized, you will change the world for good. If you aren't, if you don't learn to work together, you will be chaos personified. Besides, Georgia being my best friend in the world, it's my duty, nay, my privilege as a witch, to help make sure that you do learn to work together."

"Bravo!" Samantha said applauding.

"Great, our first step is to strip down and dance naked," Micki said.

My eyes crossed, I saw the black fog creeping in again, I felt my head roll back, and I heard Micki calling my name.

"Phoebe, Phoebe, I was kidding!"

My head returned to its rightful position, my vision cleared, and I looked right at the woman.

"You are not funny," I said.

"You didn't tell me she was so fragile," Micki said to Georgia, who shrugged with her hands out. "I'll be more careful. I didn't know she was a little fainting goat."

"I've never once fainted in my life until today. Are you telling me the rest of you are all okay?" I asked.

"To be fair," Georgia said. "I didn't have a conversation with an owl. That might have pushed me over the edge too."

"I'm not a prude!" I said. "It's not like this morning I didn't have the very thought that with a private island, one could traipse around anywhere they liked in the buff. Well, before there was a security team anyway. And that our plans will ruin that. It's just, I don't feel like I know you all well enough to dance nekkid with you. Yet."

We all shared our biggest concerns with Micki, and she made a list just as promised. It turns out I wasn't the only one having dreams, but mine seemed to be the most vivid. I also wasn't the only one with a familiar. Once Micki explained the telepathy a witch shares with her familiar, Samantha and Georgia admitted they carried on conversations with Hazel and

Venus and imagined the animal's responses. Georgia and I shared that we wanted to learn to embrace our powers and to only use them for good. And then there was the island development and Georgia's desire to complete it in supernatural time. But what was weighing on us all at the moment was Gordy's murder, and clearing Nellie's name. Samantha was able to share what she had learned while she was in Lansbury picking up Hazel.

"The police are almost convinced that we didn't have anything to do with Gordy's murder," Samantha said.

"Almost?!" Georgia and I said at the same time.

"Yeah. So the funeral director confirmed that he saw the three of us sitting at the cemetery for some time after the service ended and everyone left, but the cops said that maybe we were waiting to get word the deed was done. Apparently, having money makes you an instant suspect for hiring a hitman," she told us.

"Well, isn't that special," I said.

"I asked them to confirm the rumor I'd heard that there was a journal entry found at Gordy's that he was the one who killed Melanie, the librarian," Samantha said. "They said as soon as they find a way to confirm it wasn't coerced and was actually Gordy's handwriting, Nellie will be cleared," she said.

"How are we going to prove that?" Georgia said. "Invite him to a seance?"

"That wouldn't work because he didn't write it," I reminded her.

"I declare! If it's not one thing it's another," Georgia said rising from the table, going to the empty coffee pot, and starting a fresh pot.

"Here's the rest of what I learned through some back channels," Samantha said. "So far, the autopsy looks like Gordy died of natural causes. But they are running more tests. My source told me it looks like a heart attack, but because he was young, they are testing for all kinds of agents that can mask as heart failure. The woman who was with him swears they were coming here to pay their respects. So unless she is found to be the hired gun, that would explain why he was on the island."

"Just tell us," Georgia said. "What does it all mean? Where are we? What do we need to be concerned about?"

"I think it will all be okay," Samantha assured us. "Even if they do try to charge one of us, I have enough information to create reasonable doubt."

"I hope so, since we really didn't do it!" I said. "Now can we talk about my dream? I have a feeling something else happened on this island. There is another story buried here."

"I'm famished, and this coffee is eating a hole in my gut," Georgia said. "What if I fix us a quick lunch so we can eat and talk on the porch."

"Sounds good. I'll help with lunch," Samantha said.

"I'll set the table," I offered.

"I'll meet you out there after I use the little girl's room and freshen up from my trip," Micki said.

I gathered plates, napkins, and silverware and went out the back door to the porch that faced the ocean. As I set places on the glass and iron table, I couldn't shake the feeling of doom Sam's report left growing in my gut. Then, in my mind, I heard Sage's deep voice.

"It's going to be fine," she said.

"Yeah, I'm sure it will. But I can't stop worrying. I know Samantha was able to get Nellie out of house arrest because of her age and physical state, but that won't work for us," I said aloud to the owl.

"No, I'm telling you, I have seen the future. That's not something you need to worry about," Sage insisted. "But you're correct. There is meaning in your dreams. It's important because not only is it going to teach you much about this island, but it's also going to influence your writing. That's why I'm here. Your journey is my purpose."

"Thank you," I said aloud again.

"You're welcome, but I haven't done anything yet," Micki said behind me. I startled. "You weren't talking to me, where you?"

"Actually, no, but if I had known you were there, I would have thanked you too," I said.

Micki and Samantha came out carrying a platter of finger sandwiches garnished with crudites and a bowl of chopped fruit.

"I can't wait to hear about your dreams," Georgia said.

I looked at the three women sitting around me. I thought about the two cases we were still trying to get answers to, the case of the dead librarian, and the case of the dead driver. I suspected I was about to share the beginning details of another death.

CHAPTER TWELVE

"I understand your family's particular gift is mediumship, being able to see and communicate with spirits of both the dead and the living, right?" Micki asked.

"Yes, that's right," Samantha said as we all dug into our light lunch.

"Perfect, do you know if anyone has additional gifts?" Micki asked.

"My mom and I have been able to see things in dreams," Samantha said. "We've dabbled a bit in lightwork, some spell work, and my mom fancies herself a kitchen witch."

"Um," I said. "What is lightwork? And by the way, if I'm in the kitchen, there's likely not any witchcraft going on. Unless it's surviving my cooking."

"Lightworkers are very intuitive people, and healers," Georgia said. "They are able to feel what others need and direct their energy and healing powers to them."

"And Georgia," Micki said. "what about you? What powers have you been using unaware of your gift as a medium?"

"As you know, I've been practicing shamanism. Using ancient traditions grounded in nature to communicate with past spirits and the universe to heal others and myself."

"Phoebe," Micki said. "What about you?"

"My superpower is watching TV shows about witches," I said. "And reading. Though I tend to read more mysteries than fantasy. But now that you mention it, since I was a little girl, preteen probably, I've had déjà vu dreams. I would dream about conversations or being in a place months or years before it happened. I never remembered the dreams until the event happened, but then I would recall that I had dreamed about it. I told a few people, and they assured me everyone does that."

"That's true," Micki said. "Everyone has the ability to be a medium. But it has to be honed to be able to control it so it can serve a purpose. First, you must believe in it. Second, if you want something intentional to happen, you must do something to make it happen. And third, you need to train your mind to remember it after you wake. Now, show of hands, how many of you have been having active dreams recently?"

All three of our hands shot up, and my mouth fell open. Here I thought I was the only one. Were they dreaming about the same thing I was, or something different?

"Perfect, let's dig in. Who wants to start?"

We looked at one another. I was happy to start, I'd been waiting all morning to share my dream about the woman on the beach. But now I wanted to hear what everyone else was dreaming about.

Samantha said, "I'll go first. The night that Nellie died, I had a dream about what happened to the librarian. But to be honest, at the end of the dream I saw Nellie walking into her mother's embrace. When I woke up, I knew she was gone, and I forgot about the rest of the dream. Since then, I've had dreams about the family, who all the players are, what went wrong, who killed Melanie the librarian, and why."

"Do you feel you have a true and accurate account of the events? " Micki asked her.

"I do. I've been able to see them from different perspectives, and I believe them to be true. That's why I had the sentinels leave evidence at Gordy's confessing the murder of the librarian. He killed her."

"Okay, good. Let's get a feel for what everyone is seeing and then we can lay things out. What do you think?"

We all nodded in agreement.

"I've been dreaming about Grand," Georgia said. "She's been helping me plan the island and occasionally dropping hints about what happened before she died too."

"So that's how you had all those plans about the island so quickly?" I asked.

"Of course. I'm a librarian, not a developer," Georgia answered, laughing.

"I for one feel so much better!" I said. "I loved our game of 'Yes And' but,' I was intimidated by your plans. Here I thought you were brilliant. A genius. One of those people who are good at everything!" I said.

"No," Samantha said. "I'm the one who is good at everything." We all laughed.

"Phoebe, you raised your hand. Do you know what you have been dreaming about?" Micki asked.

"I usually don't remember my dreams," I said. "But ever since arriving at the island I've had the most vivid dreams. I mean full color. I've been dreaming about a woman that I think may have died on the island."

Everyone looked at me.

"You mean Grand?" Georgia asked.

"I don't think so. It's a young woman," I said.

"This island has been owned by the Hadley family for a very long time," Georgia said. "Grand told me that the ancestors used to come here to vacation. It was their camping spot of sorts. There wasn't a house here though until she built Hadley Manor. Maybe someone long ago."

"I don't think so," I said.

"Why?" Samantha asked.

"Because the woman looks like she walked out the '80s. Farrah hairdo, a navy sailor dress with white piping, and I've seen Hadley Manor in the dream too."

"Let's vote," Micki said. "Which dream do we want to start with?"

"Phoebe's," everyone said at once. Except me. I wanted to hear them all.

"Okay, Phoebe," Micki said, acting as the orchestrator. "Tell us what you know."

I shared with them the dream. How at first it was like I was looking down on the woman, and then that I was following her and ending with the piece of the dress I found under the bolder near the lake.

Georgia asked for a description, I told her all I could remember. Micki asked if the woman tried to communicate with me. I said no.

"Is there a lake on the island?" Samantha asked. "I haven't seen one."

"There is," Georgia said. "I forgot all about it. On the undeveloped part of the island not far from the lighthouse. Grand always wanted to build a pier on the lake, and I never understood why. She said she just always wanted a pier on a lake."

"What did you do with the scrap of fabric from the dress, Phoebe? Did you bring it back with you?" Micki asked.

"No. I put it back where I found it. I'm not really sure why, now that I think about it," I said.

"Because you followed your intuition, and you intuitively knew that changing something could alter everything else. That's the first lesson in being a witch. Even though we have the power to manipulate things, when we do, we must understand that even the smallest thing can have big ripples. Just like casting a rock into water. The ripples are small where the rock goes in and it doesn't seem to make big waves, but each one reaches further and further out."

"I wish I knew her name," I said.

"Ask her!" Micki said.

"Seriously? It's that easy? How do I make myself do that in a dream?" I asked.

"I can help with that," Micki said. "Before bed, I can show you how."

"I want to know who she is too!" Georgia said. "Grand entertained a lot of people on the island. But most were fellow authors. There weren't many women in those days. I don't recall anyone who looked like Farrah, but if it was the '80s, it might have been while I was away at college."

"Wait," Samantha said. "You said your dreams have changed since you've been here?"

"Yes. I used to never remember them," I said. "Usually sometime later when an event happened that I had dreamed about before. But here they are clear and colorful, and I remember them completely. I notice small details. Now that I think about it, even sensory details. The feeling of wind, the smell and sound of the ocean, are all vivid."

"I wonder if Nellie spelled her room!" Micki said.

Samantha stood up from the table and went inside. We all followed her.

"What kind of spell," I asked, trying hard to not freak out, but the creepy crawlies were running up and down my spine, my arms, even my legs. I felt like I had just walked through a ginormous spider web and was frantically fighting back the urge to break into a ninja dance to rid myself of it.

"It could be a spell or an enhancement," Micki said.

We were all standing in the hall outside Nellie's room, peering in.

"Micki," Samantha said, "if it was a spell, would you be able to feel it if you walk in there?"

"It's possible. Want me to go first?"

"I might be able to," Samantha said. "I've thought I felt one before, but I'm too new at this to trust it. You may be more intuitive. If you don't mind. But I understand if you don't want to go in there alone."

"Don't be silly," Micki said. "I'm not afraid. Phoebe's been sleeping in there, and she's still alive."

Georgia, Sam, and I looked wide-eyed at Micki remembering that Nellie did die in that room.

Micki laughed. "I'm kidding, girls, relax!" she said.

"Oh, she doesn't know," Georgia said.

"She doesn't know what?" Micki asked.

"That Grand died in there, in her sleep."

Micki froze. Literally, froze in an absurd position. Her face frozen in a look of shock and surprise, her arms at weird angles as they were naturally swinging before the freeze. It looked like the way it does on TV when they freeze someone. But her eyes were still blinking.

Then Sam, Georgia, and I all laughed.

"You're kidding?" Micki asked relaxing.

"No. Not at all. She did die in here in her sleep. But it wasn't because of a spell," Georgia said.

"How do you know?" Samantha asked. "Did she tell you in a dream?"

"No. Because Phoebe's been sleeping in there and she's fine." Georgia said with a grin.

"Wait. You put me in there to sleep because I might have died?"

"No way, silly!" Georgia reassured me. "I definitely don't need another body popping up on this island any time soon! I didn't know about any spell. I just thought I wouldn't be able to sleep in there because it was Grand's room. And Samantha had already stayed in another room. It just was logical," she insisted.

"Right. Stick the poor relation in the deadly death chamber room," I said, my snark creeping out again.

"Oh, my, this is going to be fun." Micki said with a chuckle, and she walked into the room.

"I don't feel anything," she said. "Come on in and let's see what we can find," Micki said.

"What are we looking for?" Georgia asked. "Also, Nancy cleaned this room, changed the bedding, all that after Grand died. Is it possible she moved, removed, or cleaned away a spell or enchantment?"

"Herbs, crystals, candles can all be used. It's likely not candles unless Phoebe lit them," Micki said.

"No," I said. "I haven't lit any."

"You mean like this?" Georgia said pointing to a vase of what appeared to me to be wildflowers that was on the bedside table.

"Exactly like that!" Micki said. "Those are mugwort, valerian, and yarrow. Together they would help enhance dreams and memory of them, but usually when consumed in tea form. On the bedside they might have some affect, but not like what Phoebe is describing."

I looked up to see Samantha unmaking the bed, carefully pulling back one layer at a time and inspecting it. There was nothing there, but I was wondering how well I was going to sleep that night. When she got to the bed pillows and lifted the pillow I had been sleeping on, the sunlight caught a beautiful crystal and it sparkled. The crystal was a deep purple in color on one end, fading to almost white on the other, about 3.5 inches long and about 2 inches wide. with three sides. It looked not unlike a purple diamond, faceted on all three sides, with three points.

"Amethyst!" Micki said. "That's it."

"How have I not felt a rock under my pillow?" I asked perplexed.

"Are ye a princess, my girl?" Georgia asked.

"Yeah, okay, I deserve that after my plucking Venus from the sky snark. But no, not a princess, but normally a light sleeper."

"An amethyst under the pillow will feel flat and light as a feather to a witch," Micki explained.

"Well, there's one mystery solved," Georgia said. "Shall we remake this bed? Do you want to keep the crystal under the pillow, Phoebe?"

"Yes, please, that's about as cool as iced sweet tea with mint!"

"Afterwards, why don't we take Micki on a tour of the island so we can discuss plans for an author community?" Georgia asked. "I need to lighten up a bit.

We all agreed.

Before bed that night, Micki invited us to the beach where she built a fire. She invited us to stand around the fire, and she gave us each a printed sheet of paper. "Here's a spell I wrote to help you in your dream states. Let's all read it aloud together."

"By the light of the silver moon,
In dreams, we shall meet soon.
With this spell, I shall travel deep,
Into thy dreams, I shall take this leap.
I call upon the spirits of night,
Guide me through the slumbering sight.
With magic words, I cast this spell,
To enter the realm of dream's sweet well.
I seek to enter thy dreaming mind,
And speak with thee of visions kind.
With this spell, our minds shall meld,
And our conversation shall be held.
Dreams, open up thy hidden gate,
Let me pass through without debate.
I seek the one who is sleeping sound,
And with this spell, I shall be found.
By the power of the witches craft,
I enter the dream realm at last.
To speak with thee, and to impart,

A message that is deep in my heart.
As I will, so mote it be."

Chapter Thirteen

The next morning, I awoke with a pounding headache. I wasn't sure if it was my headache or Rosemary's. Yes, the lady who had been appearing in my dreams told me that her name was Rosemary. And she implored me to help her. She said I was the only one who could. I heard a familiar screech outside my door. Yes, pun intended. I knew instantly that it was Sage. I stood up gently from the bed, the headache intense, and opened the door to the balcony and a gentle spring rainfall.

Sage was perched on the balcony rail again, and I was surprised to see no rain falling on the terrace outside my room. I glanced up and noticed that there was also a balcony on the third floor that created a protective overhang, and I thought how lovely it would be to sit out and enjoy a coffee in the rain. It also reminded me that we hadn't been back to the attic since finding Gordy's body, bless his heart, may he rest in peace. And that further reminded me that we never got around to Samantha's dreams the day before about what happened before we arrived on this island.

"It's a lot," Sage said. She was speaking aloud, and I much preferred it.

"I'm sorry. What is?" I asked.

"Everything that's happened since you arrived," Sage answered. "Are you journaling it all?"

"No. Maybe that's contributing to the out-of-sorts feeling I have. I usually journal every morning. But I didn't bring my journal."

"Not a problem!" Sage said. "In the bedroom, go to the small chest next to the bathroom. Open the bottom drawer."

"Okay, why?"

"Go ahead, now," said the owl.

"Bossy much?" I asked.

"Testing your hearing ..." it snarked back. I left the door open while I went inside to open the drawer. It made me feel uneasy to think about opening Nellie's chest. It felt like an invasion of privacy.

"Nellie's gone. Nothing here belongs to her anymore," Sage said. "And if she were here, she would offer that drawer to you with pleasure."

I pulled the drawer handles. It was heavy and a bit stubborn. Inside I found that it was full of unused red leather journals plus 3 boxes of writing pens.

"Go ahead. Take one," Sage said. "Before you go downstairs this morning, write down everything you can remember from your dreams. It will be important to remember all that you can."

"Why? What can you see, Sage? Apparently, you saw me coming here, and now it sounds like you can see the future too."

"I can see much on both sides of the veil," the owl said.

"By the veil, you mean those alive and those who aren't, right?"

"Yes, that is correct. I cannot see far future, but I can see near future as it pertains to my charge. If there's any confusion, that means you."

"What exactly is near future? Hours, days, years?"

"Sometimes I can't see the amount of time, but not years. Listen to me, danger is coming. You must solve Rosemary's death to protect not only yourself, but Georgia and Samantha too. Micki will help you, Rosemary will help as much as she can, but the three of you are going to have to do the heavy lifting on this."

"Are you telling me that Rosemary was murdered?" I asked. I knew. I just wanted confirmation. This whole thing about my dreams being a factual historical documentary was, well, not normal. I didn't care what people said. Really not normal.

"You've already seen that, haven't you," Sage said.

"You're a wise old, um, hoot. By the way, would it be insensitive to ask if you're a girl owl or a boy owl?"

"Why would that be insensitive?" Sage asked. I noticed it wasn't an answer to my question.

"These days, it can be a sensitive question. We've assigned so many roles and stigmas based on gender that humans are tired of it. It seems there's a mass movement to disassociate with gender altogether," I said.

"Yes, I get it. In the human world, men have been considered superior in every way for millennia. In the natural world, the female is considered the ruler of all things. We are not dominated." Sage said.

"Aha! So you are a girl!" I said.

"And why do you think that?" Sage said.

"Because you said, 'We are not dominated.' That would mean you are part of we, therefore a girl," I explained.

"Excellent. You have the ability to discern fine details and deduce logical conclusions. Now, hurry. There's no time to waste," Sage flew away. I looked down at the journal in my hand, and I went back to the drawer for a pen. I sat in a chair on the balcony and wrote all the details I could think of from my dreams, and I made a list of questions I had because of them. Then I showered, dressed, and went to the kitchen for a much-needed cup of coffee, carrying the journal with my notes.

Samantha and Georgia were already at the table. On the bar there was a large empty coffee mug waiting to be filled. After we all said good morning, I reached for the mug, and when I lifted it, I realized it felt heavier than it should be. I looked down.

"Ahhh!" I screamed and tossed the mug and then frantically tried to catch it again. The journal I was carrying in the other hand flew across the room. I succeeded in catching the mug before it crashed onto the floor.

Georgia and Samantha were roaring with laughter.

"What the..." I said looking into the fur filled mug.

Samantha reached to take the mug from me. She turned it up on its side and the quill covered creature slid out into her hand.

"Meet Hazel," Samantha said. "I'm sorry she startled you. I brought her down out of her habitat for a bit, and I needed to set her down. I put her in the mug because the slick sides would keep her from escaping until I take her back upstairs. I'm sorry."

Micki came through the entrance of the kitchen.

"Now that was funny!" she said.

"You were here too?" I asked.

"In the little girl's room. I heard it all and imagined the sight. Don't spoil it for me by telling me what really happened. In my imagination it was glorious, and it will be a scene in an upcoming book," she said.

"Get some coffee," Georgia said, finally getting her laughter under control. "We need to talk."

"No joke," I said. "Sage just scared the bejesus out of me."

"Sage?" Micki asked. "You mean Hazel?"

"Well, yeah, Hazel too. But my snarky bossy familiar scared me even more," I said. "She thinks we are in danger, and we have to solve Rosemary's murder to avert said peril," I shared.

"Her name is Rosemary? The woman on the beach?"

"Yes, her name is Rosemary," I shared. "The year was 1983. And something bad happened on this island."

"I know," Georgia and Samantha said at the same time.

"Wait. How do you know?" I said, looking at them both confused.

It turns out they both dreamed about Rosemary that night. But we all saw it from different points of view. I saw and felt what Rosemary felt, Georgia saw and felt what the killer felt, and Samantha saw it through the eyes of a witness.

"Well, that tells us more, doesn't it," Micki said. "Now we know the year, and it's clearly within the time Nellie lived on the island, but we also know that there were at least two other people on the island that night."

"You know what? There's something familiar about it too," Georgia said. Didn't the sentinels say that Gordy and his date came to the island by boat and came ashore by the lighthouse?"

"Yes," Samantha answered.

"In my dream, I came ashore on a boat by the lighthouse," Georgia said. "Maybe Grand didn't know this Rosemary person. Maybe she was the friend or a date of someone trespassing. I know someone else was in that boat with me."

"Are you sure?" I asked. "Or are you floating above the person in the boat?"

"She's sure," Samantha said. "Because in my dream I too came in a boat with someone else."

"Is it possible you two were dreaming about the same person?" Micki asked.

"I dreamed about a struggle with Rosemary," Georgia said. "I pushed her, and she hit her head on a rock."

Samantha gasped. "I dreamed I saw someone, a man, shove the woman, she hit her head on a rock, and then I helped that man toss her into the lake."

"Confirmed," I said. "There were three people at the lake that night. Now we just have to figure out who they were. What happened to my journal?" I asked, remembering my notes.

"It went flying when you found Hazel," Samantha said and pointed to the other side of the room where the book lay on the floor. I went to pick it up.

"Hey, that looks just like Grand's journals," Georgia said.

"Confession, it is a new journal out of Nellie's drawer in her bedroom," I explained. "Sage told me to get it because I left mine in Texas, and she told me to write everything I remember and any questions I have from the dream. She said Nellie wouldn't mind, and I think that's true. But I didn't think about asking you. I'm sorry."

"Don't be silly!" Georgia said. "It's given me a fantastic idea. We need to go find Grand's journals from that year. If she knew Rosemary, it will be in the journal. If she knew what happened that night, it will be in there too."

"Oh! Great idea," Samantha said.

There was a knock on the front door.

"I keep forgetting to tell the security team to let us know when someone is coming!" Georgia said. "All this talk about people coming by boat and other people ending up dead has me rattled."

"I'll get it," Samantha said.

Georgia, Micki, and I sat in silence and listened while Samantha went to answer the door. Absurdly, I picked up the large mug that held Hazel and found myself holding the mug against my chest and stroking it as though I was petting Hazel. I missed my dog. We heard two female voices talking to Samantha approaching the kitchen. The voices were vaguely familiar to me, but Georgia clearly recognized them.

"Nancy and Cindy!" she exclaimed. I remembered they were Nellie's housekeepers and wondered why they were here. To my knowledge, no one asked them to come.

"What are you doing here? This is a nice surprise!" Georgia said, standing and hugging the two women. "Sit, have a seat, can I get you some coffee?"

"We're sorry for coming unannounced," Nancy said. "But we were up all night hashing out an idea, and our excitement got the better of us," she explained as Cindy motioned for Georgia to sit and went to pour her sister and herself coffee and start a new pot. I noticed she was carrying a basket, like a picnic basket, and wondered if they brought food. I was famished.

"First, we brought you some breakfast. I wasn't sure what might or might not be in the house, so we prepared it and brought it with us," Nancy said.

"We have enough lunches and dinners for a fortnight at least," Georgia said, "but not much in the way of breakfast foods. We've kind of been skipping breakfast. Let me introduce you to my longtime friend Micki. Micki, please meet Nancy and Cindy, sisters who took the absolute best care of my Grand."

"We haven't exactly skipped breakfast. We were just drinking breakfast," I said, holding up the mug I was clutching to my chest and remembered it held the tiny little mammal. I handed the Hazel-containing mug to Samantha, and Cindy came and set plates in front of us with muffins, fruit, and quiche still warm from the oven.

I took one bite of the quiche and exclaimed, "Oh, my gosh, I'm in heaven. I am starving," I said.

"It wasn't entirely a selfish act," Nancy said. "We would like to make a proposal if we may. I can explain it while you're eating, and then we can discuss it when you're done. Would that be okay?"

"Yes, of course. Please proceed," Georgia said between bites.

"Cindy and I were so shocked by Nellie's generous gift to us that we didn't even know what to think," Nancy began. "But over the last couple of days, we've been talking about what our best lives would look like. We've dreamed of exotic vacations, moving abroad, all sorts of things. But what we finally realized is that we can't imagine our lives away from Paisley Island. Since we know that you may be considering opening a B&B for authors, we wondered if we might be able to invest and be part of it. We could run the breakfast side, even offer light lunches. We could also do the cleaning. But before you say no, please understand that Nellie never made us feel like hired help. We were passionate about helping her and considered her a friend. So if our investment can help, we want to help. We thought that if you didn't have plans for the carriage house garage, we could convert it into a cafe."

"Sis, take a breath," Cindy said. "We know you need some time to think about it, and you may not even be thinking about that right now, but we wanted you to know that we're interested. We don't expect an answer today. And we would love to hear more about your plans when you have the chance to solidify them."

"We are starting to make some plans, though we haven't solidified anything yet," Georgia said. "I know I am not the person to prepare meals every day for guests and residents. Samantha? Phoebe?"

"You know I'm all in on building the community and helping in any way that I can, but I thought I would continue my law practice," Samantha said. "I never really saw myself as part of the daily operations."

"Phoebe?" Georgia asked.

"I'm perfectly happy to help with the operations, but you don't want me serving breakfast unless it's toaster waffles and pizza leftovers. I'm a hot disaster in a kitchen," I confessed. "I'm happy to take reservations, conduct tours, dust, and strip beds, but the kitchen is not my domain."

Georgia then explained to the ladies her vision, which we all now knew was actually Nellie's vision shared in the dreamworld from beyond the veil, to build the island into a permanent residence community.

"That sounds amazing and just what Nellie would have loved," Nancy said. "We'll leave you to think about it and discuss it, and if you think we would be a good fit, just let us know."

Georgia looked really thoughtful for a moment as the ladies were standing up to leave.

"Do either of you know about a crystal we found under Grand's pillow?" Georgia asked.

The sisters looked at each other before Nancy spoke. "Yes. Nellie was a forward thinker and held some esoteric beliefs and knowledge from another time. It wasn't anything we ever talked about. But when I found the crystal under her pillow on the same day that she asked me to help her gather some herbs from the gardens, I knew."

"What do you mean, you knew?" Georgia asked.

A shared glance between the sisters had Georgia prodding more, "It's okay. You can tell me, tell us, anything. Nothing you can say is going to surprise us, I promise."

"We knew that Nellie was a witch," Nancy said with a sigh. She looked like she'd just had to inform us that our dearly beloved was a serial killer.

"And how did you come to this conclusion?" the attorney among us asked.

"Because we're witches," Cindy confessed. The sisters looked as though the excitement about their proposed business alliance drained out through their feet from the shocking confession.

"Woo-hoo!" I yelled, launching from my chair and throwing my hands up. Georgia and Sam's responses were much more dignified but meant the same thing. Samantha also jumped up from her chair and hugged the two sisters, Georgia clapped and smiled, and Micki got up and danced.

"Wait," Nancy said. "So you knew?"

"I didn't know until after the funeral," Georgia said. "But so many more things make sense now."

"I'm so relieved!" Nancy said. "I was terrified that if you knew, you wouldn't want us here. But even though we've never lived on the island, it feels like home."

"I don't know," I said. "Wait just one holy minute. Did you two spell that breakfast to make us say yes?"

"What?" Cindy asked a look of total confusion on her face. "No, of course not."

I laughed, then Georgia, Sam, and Micki laughed too.

"If you want to be in cahoots with us, we need to know you've got the ability to handle some humor, ladies." I said.

"Girls, can we huddle over there," Georgia said, pointing to the back door. Samantha and I nodded.

"I might have some input," Micki said. "If it's okay to join you?"

We waved her over and we stood in a circle, leaned in where our heads were all touching and whispered. We broke the huddle and walked solemnly back to the table. Nancy and Cindy were clearing the dishes and packing up to go home.

"Go home," Georgia said. "And start drawing up plans for the carriage house and making menus and researching suppliers. You're in!"

We folded into a big group hug, and Georgia walked them to the door. Once the door closed behind our new partners, Georgia yelled, "Girls! The journals. Let's go!" But when she turned, we were already standing at the base of the stairs.

CHAPTER FOURTEEN

We resisted the urge to run up the stairs like teen girls racing to answer a telephone, and walked up like the dignified women we were.

"Georgia," I asked, "what was it like here when Nellie was alive? Especially when you were younger, I mean."

"I always thought it was magical," Georgia said. "Not the magical way we are experiencing now. But my fondest memories are of sitting here in this study with Grand and her friends. She called herself an introvert, but it seemed to me there were almost always people around. I understand now that they were her community. Each person hand selected, invited in, and trusted; she was comfortable in their company. They shared interests and talents.

"The men and women who sat in this study smoking cigars and cigarettes - in an age where that was a popular thing to do - and sipping cognac, were names that in my adulthood would be revered. Names such as Salinger, Bradbury, Vonnegut, Puzo, and Adams were like family to me. I sat in the leather chairs in dresses, knee socks, and Mary Janes, and listened to them talk about characters, who might get a movie deal, and the state of the world. I remember being quiet as a mouse so I would be allowed to stay to listen, and I loved the smells of the smoke, the first edition leather-bound books, and the cologne.

"Grand was especially fond of the few women in the industry at the time. We talked with Harper Lee, Margaret Atwood, and Anne Rice. She respected them, and told me they were good role models for me. But I didn't have the talent. Not the talent to create stories and write them. Not even the talent to tell a good story."

"I would have killed to be in this room with them," I said. "My father was the one who supported my dream to become a writer. But my dream died when he did."

"It wasn't all rosy," Georgia said. "My grandparents divorced in 1966, a year after my father was killed in Vietnam. The divorce was scandalous at the time, and we didn't talk about it. Ever. So I hardly remember him. My mother never recovered from my dad's death. Maybe because Grand took care of us financially and Mom didn't have to move on with her life, she seemed to stagnate. She seemed vacant all the time. She kept the house clean, put meals on the table, attended my school programs, and walked on the beach. Those were the only signs of life. She spoke only when necessary and then, when I was older, would tell me stories of my dad. By her accounts, it was an epic, maybe even legendary love. She never said the words, but I always felt she wished she had died with him. I don't blame her. At least, not now I don't.

"So, the fact that she let me spend my weekends, summers, and school holidays with the old eccentric grandmother was good. I liked it. For me, it was the best place I could be. Even as a teenager, I would rather spend the weekend with my grandmother than with friends. It never occurred to me that I might be an introvert too. After spending so much time in that study listening to educated adults, teenage girls seemed so silly and boring to me."

"It does sound a little like a fairy tale. A bittersweet one for sure," I said. "I'm sorry you didn't get to know your dad."

"It's okay. I think it was probably easier than you losing yours," she answered. "My reading lessons with Grand were from these autographed first editions of the American greats. Fitzgerald, Faulkner, Steinbeck. We talked not only about the stories and poems, but of the process and how the world influenced writers. I had everything a girl could need to become a literary great, and I always suspected it's what she wanted from me. But she never once seemed disappointed in me. She taught me the love of a good book. I think I was destined to become a librarian. She sent me to college and that's exactly what I did. In 1983, I was a Junior at Duke. Here they are!"

During her story, Georgia had been scanning a set of secret bookcases, behind the bookcases you could see in the library study. There were nearly as many journals as there were books. She pulled eight red leather-bound journals from the shelf. Each one had a white label attached with a handwritten year and a number in parentheses.

"Grand never had a shortage of words," Georgia said. "If we split these up, we can get through them faster. Look for references to Rosemary. I plan to skim them because, if I start reading them, I'll be here for years lost in memories. But feel free to do as you like."

We all sat in the comfortable library, Georgia opened all the blinds to allow natural light in, and we started reading. Georgia took the first two journals of the year, I took the second two, Samantha took the next two and Micki took the last two. It was so hard not to read every line. It was also hard to read the handwriting until I got used to it, but my desire to find out what happened to Rosemary was more urgent than my desire to learn more about this famous aunt of mine. There would be time for that later.

After only a few minutes, Georgia went back to the hidden bookcase and pulled more journals from further back in history.

"Grand knew Rosemary for sure. She's all through this journal. But I don't know who she is. I'm going back to find where she first appears and how exactly she came into Grand's life. Are you seeing her mentioned in your journals?"

"Yes," I answered.

"Yes," Samantha answered.

"No," Micki answered.

"Okay!" I said excitedly. "So we know Rosemary died somewhere between Samantha's book and Micki's!"

I grabbed the second book in front of Samantha. We both were flipping pages scanning for Rosemary's name.

Georgia stood at the bookcase pulling a journal, flipping through it, then replacing it, pulling another and repeating.

"I found it!" Georgia said.

"Here it is!" I yelled.

"Start at the beginning," Micki said. "Georgia, who was she?"

Georgia's eyes were rapidly scanning pages while she walked back towards us.

"Apparently, after I left for college, Grand found herself lonely and depressed," Georgia said. "She never told me. I could have come back on weekends, if she had. She always seemed so excited for me to be away and on my own. I missed her too, but I thought she would be disappointed if I came home too often. Anyway, she hired Rosemary to be her assistant. It doesn't say what her duties were to be, but I think she was really just a companion. She was my replacement," Georgia said shutting the journal.

"Not your replacement," Micki said. "Your placeholder, your substitute. No one could have ever replaced you in your grandmother's life."

Georgia nodded, "What did you find Phoebe?"

I read aloud from the journal.

"Rosemary didn't show up today. That's not like her. In three years, she's never not shown up. No phone call, no explanation. I'm worried about her. Yesterday she said she was going to walk on the beach and then go home. I'm going out to look for her," I read, turning the page. "This entry is dated the next day and says, 'I think Rosemary left my employment. I don't understand. Well, I do, after much thought. She was a young girl and being secluded on this island day in and day out is no life for a young girl. It's why I wanted Georgia to go away to college while selfishly I didn't want her to leave at all. Rosemary seemed distant and moody lately. I felt like something was bothering her, but I didn't want to push her. I thought she knew she could talk to me about anything, and I expected that she would when she was ready. Instead, she left that night and disappeared. I've tried calling her but don't get an answer. Yesterday, I called the police department and explained that I was afraid something happened to her. They all but laughed at me. They said she probably ran off with a man and maybe they're right.'"

"What's the date of that entry?" Micki asked.

"May 7th, 1983," I answered.

Micki consulted her phone. "The moon phases from 1983 are the same as this year. That means that tomorrow night, the moon will be exactly the same as the night Rosemary went missing. If we follow the paths of your dreams, we should be able to see exactly the same as they did that night."

"Should we go in the daylight?" Georgia asked. "Won't we be able to see more?"

"Maybe," Samantha said. "But we might also disturb evidence."

"How much evidence can be left after forty years?" Georgia asked.

"A scrap of cotton/poly blend fabric has survived," I reminded them.

"I have an idea," Micki said. "Let's go there now, I want to look around and plan. Tonight, we'll go back prepared. I might need to look in the attic for some things. Would that be okay?"

"Yes. Okay, let's go."

Chapter Fifteen

The four of us set out like explorers without a plan. We walked the path I'd watched Rosemary walk every night since my arrival at the island, and that I had walked the other day. I asked the others what they saw and felt in their dreams the night before.

"Usually when I dream about Rosemary, I'm watching her from behind," I said. "Sometimes she will turn and look at me, talk to me, or motion to me. Last night after Micki's spell, it was like I was Rosemary. As I walked towards the lake, I felt sad. I don't know what caused the sadness, I didn't have her thoughts, only her emotion. I heard someone yelling at me, but I couldn't comprehend the words, and I felt someone shove me, then my head hit something, and it went dark. That was the end. Can you share what you saw, heard, or felt?"

"It felt like I was in someone else's body," Samantha said. "Like you said, I was someone else. I saw the whole thing happen. We arrived by boat to the island, and we were walking towards Rosemary on the beach. She didn't seem to see us, so we followed her to the lake. I was with a young man, probably in his early twenties, longish light brown hair, thin, and as we approached her, she saw him. She seemed to know him, and asked what he was doing here. He was snide, slimy, and said he heard her calling to him. He knew she was attracted to him, and they argued. He reached out and grabbed her arm. She kneed him, and he shoved her away. When he did, her head hit the boulder and she died. He didn't mean to hurt her. It was an accident."

"My dream was the same, except I was that boy," Georgia said. "We just need to figure out who he was, who I was in the dream, and where she is now. Where they both are now."

We had arrived at the lake, and I pointed out the dress scrap I found on my earlier visit. Then we all stared into the lake for a long time, thinking, and trying to envision what happened that night.

Micki broke the silence, "I think we need to have a ceremony. I'm going to write a spell for the evening, and we should return under the familiar moon to that night. We need fire, but I fear a fire here would spread with the dry grasses. We'll build it on the beach. Georgia, I don't suppose you have a drum here, do you?"

"No, and I don't recall ever seeing one in Grand's house either," she said.

"I'll check the attic when we return. If all else fails, I noticed there's a five-gallon water cooler in the house and an empty bottle would work. We'll do the ceremony on the beach right where we turned off to come to the lake, and then walk in to see if you can see more from your dreams."

"I think it's clear -" Samantha said, "-that Rosemary died that night. And that a boy killed her. Now we need to know who the two men were and where they are now. We threw her in the lake, I'm guessing the skeleton is probably still there. Once we have a body, we can contact the police."

"Are you sure that's the best thing to do?" I found myself asking. "I mean, how do we describe how we found the body, assuming we do."

"I don't know. We'll figure that out," Samantha said.

"All of this is making me wonder if we will ever be successful at building Grand's legacy community," Georgia said. Her voice sounded sad, resigned to me.

"Why?" Micki asked, alarmed.

"Well, think about it," Georgia said. turning to walk back to the manor. "Grand was arrested right before her death and that made news, a guy was found dead on the island, now another body may turn up here. This is all bad publicity. Why would anyone want to vacation or live here once it all gets out?"

"Maybe we shouldn't call the cops," I proposed. They looked at me like I was the criminal. Especially Samantha.

"And let the murderer get away with it?" Samantha asked.

"I don't know," I admitted. "I feel there are too many variables right now to make a responsible decision. Once we know all the facts, we may decide there is another way to bring the killer to justice. Who knows? This happened forty years ago, maybe he committed more acts and is in jail, maybe Karma caught up with him and he died too."

"Oh, crap. I do not want some dead murderer visiting my dream world!" Georgia said.

"Better a dead one visits your dreams than a live one shows up at the door." I asked.

"Let's just wait to see what happens," Micki counseled. "We have recourse to eradicate things from our dreams just like we can bring them into our dreams."

We returned to the attic at Hadley Manor. "What are we looking for?" I asked Micki.

"It's one of those things where I'll know it if I see it. But two things that I know I need are some kind of drum, and I'm suspecting since we found an amethyst under Nellie's pillow there may be other crystals here. Moonstone would be helpful. I'm hoping there are herbs. But if there are, they may be too old. We'll just have to see."

We spent a few hours digging through the attic and walked out with what Micki thought was a suitable score. I admit I was confused. The treasures she deemed worthy and helpful amounted to three moonstone crystals, a pair of maracas, and a rain stick. The rain stick was an authentic one, not one of the mass-produced replicas that were in every souvenir shop in Texas. This one was a true cactus tube with the needles hammered to the inside; the holes still evident.

"Georgia, I didn't find a drum. Do you know if there are spare water bottles anywhere? I'm hoping for an empty one." Micki enquired.

"Yes, Grand had several of them and they were kept in the pantry. If there isn't an empty one, we'll pour the water out and use one," Georgia said.

"Waste it?" I asked, shocked.

"Of course not, silly!" she answered me. "We can pour it out into pitchers and still use it."

While they went to research the water bottle situation, I stopped in the kitchen and looked around for something to eat. In the fridge I found leftovers from the breakfast Nancy and Cindy had brought, and I hesitated for only a moment. I thought we should save it for breakfast the next day, but I'm not known for denying my desires since I became single and childless, so I pulled it out and put the quiche in to warm. I was thinking that something that would be great for the evening return to the scene of the crime would be night vision goggles. I heard a screech and looked out the window. On the porch railing sat Sage. I opened the back door.

"You rang?" the bird said.

"No, I didn't call you." I said.

"You asked for night vision, did you not?"

"I did," I admitted, "but —"

"I brought you something," she said, pointing her beak to three feathers lying on the rail next to her. "There is one for you, Georgia, and Samantha. Use a ribbon or leather to tie one to your forehead. It will help you see at night."

"Wow, thank you, Sage. That's pretty cool!" I said, picking up the feathers. I heard the door open behind me.

"Phoebe, what are you doing?" Georgia asked.

"Georgia meet Sage. Sage, this is Georgia," I said, introducing them. Then Samantha and Micki followed.

"Everybody, this is Sage. Oh, dear, familiar. Do you have one more feather for Micki?" I asked.

"Hello, it's nice to meet you all," Sage said. "I didn't bring one for Micki, because this is not her journey. It's not her vision to see."

"Didn't I tell you she was bossy?" I said. "Thank you, Sage, for this very sacrificial personal gift to help us tonight. Will you be there?"

"Hey, don't get all sappy on me," the bird said in her deep voice. "It's not like I plucked my flight feathers for you. They were on the ground from when I molted. And as long as you are on the island, I'll always be within a hundred feet of you."

We all laughed.

"Now, if you don't need anything else, I'll be on my way back to bed. See you all later," Sage said and flew off. But not before circling and allowing us to see her beautiful white wingspan.

We returned to the kitchen, and I thought, what a waste of this big house. It seemed we were always in the kitchen or the study. I told them I was warming the quiche for a late lunch and what Sage told me about the feathers and how to use them.

"I'm glad you brought that up. Do you all have a flowy dress you can wear this evening?" Micki asked.

When Georgia and I admitted that we didn't have one here, and Samantha would need to go to her house on the mainland to get one, Micki said she had an extra that would probably fit Georgia. Samantha said she had several and asked if I would like to go with her and try one on. I agreed and after lunch we headed to the island.

At dusk, the four of us dressed in flowy bohemian maxi dresses, three of us with feathers tied to our foreheads loaded into the golf cart with our other paraphernalia and headed to the spot Micki chose to kick off the night.

Micki carved a deep five-point star in the sand, and we built a fire in the center. Micki invited the three of us to hold hands around the fire, and she stood behind us, opposite the ocean, toward the field that would lead to the lake. She held the empty water jug between her knees and beat on the bottom. I was surprised at the drum-like sound.

"This is your ceremony. I'm only here as a guide," Micki said. I heard Sage call from nearby and imagined her saying, "See, I told you so." "You'll repeat the spell after me. Then pick up your instrument in your right hand, your giving hand, and your moonstone in your left hand, the receiving hand. Then follow me, shaking your instrument to carry the rhythm and energy from the circle with us to the lake. Do you understand?"

We all agreed, and I felt us swaying to the drumbeat. We repeated the spell as Micki told us, one stanza at a time.

"By the power of the earth and sky,
We witches gather, four and nigh.

We call upon the spirits of old,
To show us the past, as we behold.

With this spell, we seek the sight,
Of past events at a location's night.
Four witches, we entwine our power,
And conjure the past in this very hour.

By the magic of the witch's call,
Our vision shall transcend the walls.
We shall see the past with clear sight,
And witness the events of that night.

Our minds shall travel back in time,
To where we seek, a specific chime.
By the power of the witch's art,
Our vision shall be as one heart.

Past events, now we shall see,
Through the eyes of the witches three.
Our spell is cast, so mote it be."

We picked up the items from the sand in front of us as Micki had instructed, and walked single file toward the lake, marching and shaking our instruments to the beat of the water bottle drum Micki carried under her arm.

When we reached the lake, Micki guided us to the side of the lake where we had a clear sight of the path we had just walked and held up her arm indicating that we should stop. She set the drum down and stopped beating it. We stopped shaking the rain stick and the maracas and the four of us linked arms. The night silence was eerie. The only sound was the waves.

We saw Rosemary approaching and then we heard voices. Male voices. Georgia gasped as the two men came into sight. We didn't break our link or speak. We just watched.

After the two unnamed and unknown men threw a lifeless body into the lake, they started walking directly towards the four of us, still standing there with linked arms. We let each other go and ran. We ran like four teenage babysitters who just got a call from inside the house, and we didn't stop until we hit the beach.

Chapter Sixteen

We stopped, gasping for breath as we looked behind us and waited to see if we were being followed. The night was suddenly clear, and I realized that it had been slightly foggy around the lake.

"We're good," Micki said, bent at the hips, hands resting on her knees, catching her breath. "We're out of the dreamtime."

"I know who that man was, the one who killed her," Georgia said.

"Could they have really hurt us?" I asked. "We were watching the past, right? They weren't real. I mean not real right now. Were we in danger?" Samantha and I stood staring at Micki.

"I don't think so," Micki said.

"You don't think so?" I yelled.

"Shhhh," Samantha said.

"What?" I said. "We're on a private island. We're the only ones here. Who exactly do you think can hear me?"

"Oh, great, so we just witnessed a murder from the past, and now we're just supposed to brush it off like it's no big deal?" Georgia snarked. "And what do you mean 'not real right now'? I don't know about you guys, but that felt pretty darn real to me."

"Well, what do you propose we do, Samantha? Go to the authorities and tell them we saw a murder happen in a dream?" I retorted. "They'll think we're crazy."

"Or worse, they'll think we did it ourselves," Micki added, her voice low and ominous.

"So what? We just do nothing? Let a murderer get away with it?" I said, crossing my arms. I could feel the anger emanating from my body.

"We don't have any evidence, ladies," Samantha said, her tone firm. "And even if we did, we don't even know if this happened in our reality or some alternate dimension. We can't just go around accusing people without any proof."

"Fine, whatever," I huffed. "But I'm not just going to forget about this. We need to figure out what happened and make sure justice is served, even if it's just in our own minds."

We stood in silence for a moment, each lost in our own thoughts. The night was still, the only sound the gentle lapping of the lake against the shore.

"I think we should meditate on this," Georgia said finally, breaking the quiet. "Maybe we can get some more information in our dreams."

"Great, more dreamtime," I muttered under her breath. "Just what I always wanted." I heard a whooshing sound and caught the flash of white flying towards us from Sage's moonlit feathers. I held out my arm. I suppose it was an instinct to give the bird a place to land.

"Now you understand why you are in danger. That man knows all of you and he knows you're here on this island," Sage said. We all stared at the owl. "Pardon the expression, but you gals are sitting ducks as long as he's alive."

"Wait," I said. "Georgia said she knows that guy, but how do the rest of us know him?"

"Everyone knows him. What's dangerous is that he knows you!" Sage repeated.

"Who is it?" I asked confused.

Georgia took a deep breath.

"This is my problem to deal with. I'll figure it out," she said.

"Why is it your problem, Georgia?" Micki asked her.

"Because I do know him," Georgia said. "Because I've worshipped him since I was a teenager. I've called him my friend, never believing for a minute he would be capable of such a thing. I need to talk to him."

"Bloody brilliant, as my British partner would say," Samantha said. "You think this doesn't affect all of us?"

"Do you really think we would let you approach a killer by yourself?" I asked.

"The girls are right," Sage said. I noticed Micki was nodding agreement. "This is something all of you must do together. But I recommend taking a day to get some sleep first."

"You were the one telling me I had to hurry, that we were in danger," I snarked at the bird.

"True," my bossy owl said, "But you've been up all night and you need your wits about you before you approach him."

"What are you talking about?" I asked. "We've only been here a short time, and we started at dusk!"

Sage lifted a wing and pointed out to horizon over the ocean. Sure enough, the sky was lightening with shades of pink, orange, and purple.

"Great," I said. "My first beautiful sunrise on the island is tainted, not with romance or peace and tranquility, but with visions of violence dancing in my head." Without a word, we all started walking back toward Hadley Manor.

"I don't know about you girls," Micki said. "But I hope I have a dreamless sleep."

"Same," I said. "Except, I really would like to know the real "why" behind the crime."

"I agree," Samantha said, "But I feel like we need to know who the other guy was. Maybe he can shed some light on the situation."

"I'm with y'all" Georgia said. "But I would like to be able to ask Grand if she had any inkling that he was evil."

"Be careful what you wish for," Sage said and flew ahead of us.

When we returned to the house, we agreed to sleep until noon and then regroup to decide how to proceed.

I removed the borrowed dress and the feather tied to my forehead, slid into my favorite sleep shirt and crawled into bed with the red leather journal and a pen. I intended to write a description of what I saw that night at the lake. And I thought I did. But I drifted off to sleep in no time and I dreamed. If I had wanted a peaceful sleep, I should have remembered the amethyst crystal that was still under my pillow.

This time I was in the boat with the two men from the lake. I realized Georgia never shared with us who the one was that she knew. He only looked vaguely familiar. More in the way of when you see a child and you think it looks like someone, but you can't quite figure out who. I watched on as the two men talked in the boat.

"What's going on with you?" the blonde man asked the brown-haired man behind the wheel of the boat.

"Nothing. Why?"

"I don't know, you've seemed angry, broody, not your usual self," the friend asked.

"I am not broody. Girls are broody. I'm just livin' my life, dude."

"Yeah, that's what they all say. But when a guy gets silent with his best friend, there's always a girl involved. Wait! Are you trying to steal my girl from me? Are you wrestling with the ancient guy code?"

"No. I'm not interested in your girl, not that there is anything wrong with her. Probably the thing I find the most perplexing is feeling a little envious of your relationship, but not her specifically."

"What? The great Jackster who swore upon bachelorhood as though it were a religion, is envious of a committed relationship? If you tell me you have the wedding bell blues, I'mma have you committed right here and now. I'll know you're an alien or imposter or something!" the blonde friend said to the driver of the boat.

"If I'm honest, I do have wedding bell blues, but not my own. I finally met a woman who would be capable of convincing me excommunication from bachelorhood might not be so bad. But I just learned her S.O. proposed."

"Oh, dude, that's harsh. Does she know you have feelings for her?"

"I don't know. I once told her I'd give her the world if she would let me. You've never seen a woman look so unimpressed. She wasn't even tempted by a famous family name, wealth, my good looks, not to mention my charm and charisma."

"You know you're my best friend, right? But charm and charisma are not words I would use to describe you. So what do you think he's got that you don't?"

"It's really messed up. He's old enough to be her father, probably even her grandfather; yeah, I think there's like a fifty-year age difference. It's just gross. I don't have a clue what he's got that I don't except an ex-wife, a granddaughter, and the girl."

The boat was drifting on the ocean, and the two men were kicked back, relaxing, and sharing a cooler full of beer. I noticed an island off to the left with a sand beach. I spotted her a moment before the men in the boat.

"Look, there she is, I'm going to see if I can talk some sense into her. I need to stop her from making the worst decision of her life," the brown-headed man declared and started the boat engine.

I could feel the wind on my face, my hair pushed back by the force of the boat speeding towards the island. He ran the boat up on the shore and jumped out. His friend followed. I was jolted back to reality by a knock on my bedroom door.

"Come in," I called out. "And whoever you are, I hope you brought coffee."

"I did," Georgia said. "I just wanted to apologize. I realized I was not very nice back there on the beach."

"No apology necessary," I said, sitting up against the headboard and accepting the giant mug of coffee Georgia offered. "I realize this is all much more personal for you than for any of the rest of us. This is a new place and new people to me, to us, while you have a lifetime of memories and connections."

She handed me a photo and explained. "That's my Grand," she said pointing to a beautiful woman in the photo. She appeared to be in her early sixties. "That's me," she said pointing to a young coed, dressed in the requisite preppy attire for the time. "And that is Jack Poe."

My eyes bugged, and I stared at the old, slightly grainy photo and tried to reconcile the young man in the photo to the one I was familiar with from television interviews and had met after Nellie's funeral. But this didn't look like that man. This guy in the photo was the spitting image of the brown-haired man in the boat.

"I have worshipped that man since I was a girl. He was the closest contemporary I had among Grand's author friends, and I was so jealous that she was mentoring him. I was jealous that he had a talent that she wanted so desperately for me to possess that I just didn't."

"Georgia," I said. "it's so clear that your grandmother adored you. That you meant everything to her for your whole life. I mean, reading in that journal about Rosemary, she was undoubtedly here solely to keep your Grand occupied while she was allowing you to find yourself, to become the woman you were meant to be."

"Yeah, I'll always regret that we never came to terms about my Peru trip. I think maybe she got over it, but I always felt like my spirituality built a wall between us. We worked around it, but we were never as open as we had always been before that. When we found out we were witches, I was angry. I couldn't believe how hypocritical she had been to deny me that. But now I understand that she just wanted to protect me. And she's still trying to protect me. I fell asleep for a short minute, and I asked her if it was possible that Jack did this thing. She said not only possible, that there was more. She told me where to look. I found the journal for the proper time she mentioned. But I don't think I can read this alone."

"I'm honored that you came to me," I said. "I'll get dressed and we can read it together."

"Well, um, about that," Georgia said. "It's true that you're the only one I woke up for this, but that's because the others are already downstairs. We didn't want to start without you."

"Well, I'm grateful for that. I'll be right down."

Chapter Seventeen

When I arrived in the kitchen, along with Georgia, Micki, and Samantha, I discovered that Nancy and Cindy were there. They served me a plate of breakfast, and I realized I was totally famished. I looked at my watch. It was lunchtime, and I recalled that we didn't eat dinner the night before. Georgia admitted that she messaged the ladies before going to bed and asked if they could bring breakfast.

"We were excited to do it," Nancy said. "We've been testing out recipes for the new cafe. And we've been incorporating a little magic into the mix. We have here a Mind & Body Frittata, Clarity Muffins, and Creativity Shortbreads. They are recipes crafted to help with what you need most, and we can't wait to see what you all think."

"Oh, um, well, that's an interesting concept," I said, longing for a good ole western omelet, steak and eggs, or maybe a blueberry muffin. But I was almost too hungry to care. Wishing I hadn't thought of tasty ribeye with a side of fried eggs, I took a bite of the Clarity muffin and had to admit that it was delicious. Original, almost, a delicate blend of spices that made me feel special, like I was in an Italian sidewalk cafe.

"I wolfed mine down like I was starving," Samantha said, "while Georgia went to wake you up. It's all good. Enjoy. But I'm done. Do you want me to read the journal aloud?" she asked Georgia.

"No, I'm fine to read it," Georgia said. "I just didn't want to read it alone."

"Okay, then we're ready whenever you are. No rush. Do it when you're ready," Micki said.

"Do you want us to leave? We would be happy to clean today while we're here." Nancy asked.

"No, you don't have to leave. You want to be our partners on the island, I think it's only fair that you know all of its secrets," Georgia said. And then she began to read.

July 3rd, 1984

After an intense conversation this morning discussing the Olympic boycott, Jack and I set off to spend the day enjoying my secret sinful pleasure. Fishing at the lake isn't considered a lady-like activity, and Jack is the only one who knows that I escape there from time to time. The sun was shining, and there was a light breeze in the air. It felt like it was going to be a great day.

We reached our favorite spot by midmorning, and after setting up our gear, we cast our lines into the water. I left Jack to watch the poles so I could walk around the lake. On the far side, I noticed something odd. Disbelieving what I thought I saw, I called out to Jack and motioned for him to come over and take a look. As I crept closer, my heart sank as I realized what I had found – it was the skeleton of Rosemary who had gone missing a year prior!

She still wore tattered remnants of what appeared to be her dress when she disappeared all those years ago. Jack wrapped his arms around me and let me cry into his chest until my tears stopped falling. He told me he was sorry for what happened and then he suggested that it would be best if no one knew about our discovery. He wisely, I suppose, counseled me that if we called the police, they would open an investigation, and since I was the only one living on the island, I would be a suspect. I'm sure it was an accident of some sort, though even my creative mind can't come up with a logical one.

Anyway, I couldn't leave her there. She deserved a proper burial. After we debated it, Jack helped me move her out of the lake, and we found a suitable place to bury her. I'm going to go back and cover her grave with the Indian Blanket flowers that were her favorites.

My heart is broken. I feel so dirty, not from the dirt and sand we dug today, but for not telling anyone. Rosemary told me she didn't have any family. I thought she was just an independent young woman and that it couldn't be true. But no report was ever filed that she was missing. I would have heard. I hope the dear girl is resting peacefully now. I don't think I'll ever be able to fish there again.

We all sat around the table watching Georgia. She was astonished that her grandmother had discovered Rosemary's body. We could feel the sadness radiating off her as she put the book down, her hands trembling slightly. Micki pulled Georgia into a hug, while Samantha and I just looked at each other in shock.

"My grandmother ... Jack ... they covered up a murder," whispered Georgia. "What kind of person does something like this?" She was beginning to unravel before our eyes, and we felt helpless to console her.

Micki finally spoke up, breaking the silence with a single word: "Justice." Her voice was steady as she suggested that we confront Jack about what happened and demand answers.

I nodded in agreement, but Samantha seemed hesitant until she remembered the dreams that we had all seen Jack murder Rosemary!

"I shudder to think what Jack would have done if he thought Grand suspected him of the murder. But I'm furious that he used her to further ensure his crime wouldn't be discovered!" Georgia said.

"Well, the way I see it, we have two options," Samantha said. "We can either discover the body while digging - the new construction would be a good excuse - and report it to the police, or we decide to carry out our own justice. I've never been a fan of vigilantes, but I'm not sure what else we can do here. We have a body now, but no way to prove who killed her. And as Jack said, the locals will jump to the conclusion that Nellie killed her."

"Let me think about this for a minute," I said. "We don't have to do anything today, do we? I mean, this is a forty-year-old crime. Another day to think about it won't hurt anything, will it?"

"I know you're right," Georgia said. "But I can't, I just can't sit on this. I'm booking a flight to Nantucket. Who's going with me?"

"I am," I said. I mean what did I have to lose? Except I was realizing that what I wanted to write about was Rosemary and her story. I couldn't miss the opportunity to get more info, could I?

"Me," Micki said. "I'm your ride or die. You can't go without me."

"Heaven help us all," Samantha said. "I'm going if for no other reason than to bail y'all out of jail."

Nancy and Cindy stood at the kitchen bar. They had not said a word through the whole thing.

"How long will you be gone?" Nancy asked.

"I don't know," Georgia said. "It depends on how it goes down, I suppose. I want to get him to confess it all."

"If we can get it recorded," I said excited, "then we would have the proof to go to the cops without any ramifications to the island."

"We can stay here, tidy up, and watch the pets until you get back," Cindy offered.

"Thank you, both. That would be wonderful, I'll call to get flights" Georgia said, picking up the old landline that was still mounted on the kitchen wall.

I heard Sage calling me from outside the kitchen window.

"Wow, it must be important," I said. "The bossy owl should be sleeping in the middle of the day." I went to the back door and opened it to see my new feathered friend perched on the porch railing.

"Hello, what brings you out in the middle of your night?" I asked.

"Phoebe, this is dangerous. Very dangerous. And with none of your familiars there to help, I have to advise against this plan."

"What's dangerous, Sage?"

"Confronting a murderer!" the owl said.

"But is he? I mean he was certainly. But he was young, it looked like a crime of passion. He's old now. Even older than us. With three of us together, we can overpower him if we need to," I reasoned, feeling the first stirrings of wondering if the bossy owl might be right.

"He's killed. A lot. I know it, I feel it. And it's much more recent than you think. You should stay here! Let this go. The natural world will get its justice for Rosemary."

"I hear you. And I wish I could," I said. "But I can't let my friends do this alone. I have to stand with them."

"You are my witch. You are the one I have to protect. I'm concerned for them too, but my loyalty is to you, and my duty is to make sure you are safe. If something happens to you, you can't complete your journey."

"I understand. I don't fault you for your concern. But I hope you understand too, this is something I have to do."

Micki opened the door. "We need to cast a spell before we go. We're going to use the attic. Are you coming?"

"Thank you, Sage. I'll be careful. I promise. May I pet you?" I asked. The owl tucked her head, and I stroked her back cherishing the feel of her soft feathers, knowing that underneath them was a strong and powerful animal. I hoped I had that kind of strength inside me.

"You do. Just call on it," Sage said, and flew away.

In the attic, Micki asked us if we thought we were ready to start casting our own spells. Samantha said she could. Georgia and I said we would try. We gathered in the middle of the floor in a circle, and Micki spread a ring of salt around us for protection. I was a little creeped out because the last time I was here, we found Gordy. And we still didn't know what had happened to him.

I'll start, and we'll take turns," Micki said. "Just do your best, focus on intention, that's the most important thing. Ready?"

We all nodded.

"By the power of the witch's call,
We gather four, strong and tall.
To seek the truth of crimes untold,

And bring justice to the bold," Micki said.

"With this spell, we evoke the truth,
And bring forth secrets from his youth.
By the power of the witch's might,
We call upon the spirits of light," Samantha said.

"Protect us, guardians of the veil,
As we seek to prevail.
Keep us safe from harm and deceit,
As we unravel the mystery, and bring the truth to meet," Georgia said.

"We call upon the elements four,
To open the doors of the criminal's core.
Let the truth be spoken loud and clear,
And let it be known to all who hear," I said.

"By the power of the witch's way,
We invoke the truth today.
May it be revealed without harm,
And justice prevail, without alarm," Samantha said.

"Protect us, guardians of the night,
As we cast this spell, with all our might.
Keep us safe, until our task is done," Micki concluded.

CHAPTER EIGHTEEN

Our flight left at 6:00 a.m. the next morning, and a little after lunch time we were in a rental car on our way to Jack Poe's estate on Nantucket. We drove for what seemed forever up a winding path that felt like we were in a dense forest.

"Georgia, have you been here before?" Samantha asked from the passenger seat.

"No. I've only ever seen Jack at Grand's house," she said.

"How do you know his address?" I inquired from the backseat.

"We've always exchanged Christmas cards, and it's an easy address to remember," she answered.

"I'm usually as up for adventure as the next girl," Micki said, "But I'd be lying if I said I wasn't uncomfortable about this place. I mean this is remote. And all these trees, the surf in the distance, would anyone even hear us scream?"

"Don't be paranoid," Georgia said. "Why would we need to scream? I've known this man practically my whole life.

He wouldn't hurt me, no more than he would have hurt Grand."

"Georgia, don't count so much on that," Samantha said, "We are 99% sure he killed Rosemary."

"That appears to have been a crime of passion and frustration," Georgia said defending the man.

"Remember in the note that Nellie left, that authors can only write what they know. This man has written some of the darkest words ever laid on paper. How do you think he can write that, describe it in such detail, if he's never seen it?"

Georgia sighed heavily before admitting that she didn't know.

"Also keep in mind that Sage was pretty freaked out that we were coming here," I reminded her. "She seems to be able to see into the future. I think we have to be cautious. Okay, ladies?"

We pulled up in front of an estate that seemed as though the house had been set on a circular clearing in a forest on a high cliff overlooking the sea. The grounds were covered in manicured lawns and vibrant gardens with beautiful trees and flowers in bloom. The house itself was a grand, white-washed two-story home with large windows and a wraparound porch. The air was filled with the sweet fragrance of freshly mowed grass, hints of fragrant jasmine and honeysuckle from the estate gardens, and an aroma of ocean spray from off in the distance. But there in the wide drive, in front of the house, was an ambulance.

Georgia pulled out of the way, at the doors of a multicar garage and slammed the rental car's ignition into park. She slung the door open as though she was going to flee the car, but then stopped and froze.

"What if we're too late?" she asked.

"Then we are," Micki said. "And there's nothing to be done about it. Let's just wait and see," she said and opened her door. She got out and leaned against the car, staring at the front door and the ambulance parked in front of it. Georgia did the same, then Samantha and I also got out of the car to wait.

The ambulance attendants came out with a stretcher, but there was no one on it. One loaded the stretcher in the back and closed the rear doors while the other got in the driver seat. She turned and saw us and waved before going to get in the passenger side of the ambulance, and we watched as it made a three-point turn and headed back down the winding driveway. Georgia marched to the front door, and we followed her like little ducklings. I think Micki, and Samantha were handling it all pretty well. But I was bringing up the rear and checking that I wasn't dreaming, that we were about to enter the luxurious home of a famous author and accuse him of murder.

Georgia knocked twice on the front door, opened it, stuck her head in and called out, "Jack? Are you here? It's Georgia Fontaine. May I come in?"

Even from the very back, I could hear her voice echoing inside the house, bouncing between the marble floors and high ceilings. We waited, holding our breath for a reply. We only heard coughing.

Georgia walked in and followed the sound. "Yes, come in," we heard Jack call out. His voice sounded weak and congested.

We discovered the man we had met barely a week before in front of Hadley Manor lying in a hospital bed in a vast living room. The bed was positioned facing a wall of windows that looked out to a wall of trees with the ocean on the horizon. In a weird twist, the sky that had seemed sunny and bright outside suddenly seemed dark and ominous and I realized there was some sort of weird tinting on the windows to create the eerie cast both inside and out.

"To what do I owe the pleasure?" he said weakly. The four of us encircled his bed so that he could see us.

"Did I die already? I just got here," he said with a weird chuckle followed by coughing.

"Jack," Georgia said. "What's going on? What's wrong?"

"I'm dying, that's what," he said.

"We just saw you a few days ago and you seemed fine," she said.

"Yeah, I know. I was fine, at least I thought I was, a few days ago. But when I got back from Nellie's funeral, I was having trouble breathing. I stopped at the hospital, and I've been there ever since. There's nothing else they can do for me. Stage four cancer they said. They sent me home to die. And the first thing that happened is my bed is surrounded by four beautiful women. So I ask again, am I dead already? I mean, here I am without the strength to do a thing about it."

The hum of an oxygen concentrator was distracting to me. The others didn't seem to notice it, but it was a deafening roar to me.

"You aren't dead," Georgia said. "We're here because we want to talk to you about Rosemary."

"Rosemary?" he asked.

"Let me refresh your memory," Georgia said. "Summer of 1983, you and another man trespassed on Paisley Island and killed a young woman for no apparent reason. Then you tossed her into a lake and left her. A year later, you're fishing there with Grand and she discovers the body and you convince her to bury it. Sound familiar?"

"It does. It's the plotline of my book, *One Bitter Night*," he answered.

"It's more than a book and you know it!" Georgia spat. The normally calm and composed woman was starting to lose it. Her face was red, and I noticed her hands were shaking. Not from fear but extreme anger. "How could you do that to her?"

"Who? Rosemary or Nellie? What are you really mad about, Georgia?" Jack asked her. "Nellie was a teacher, a good one, but I don't owe her anything."

Georgia stood there in disbelief. Her mouth open but silent.

"Hi, Jack. I don't know if you remember me from Nellie's funeral. I'm Samantha. Do I understand correctly that you wrote a book about killing Rosemary?"

"Yes. I did. I'm not sure why you all are delusional and suddenly think it's real."

"Because we saw it," I blurted. I've been offended by men before. All my life really, at least ever since my dad died. But I was done taking it.

"You expect me to believe that the four of you were on that island forty years ago and you saw a murder that you now want to pin on me? All this time later? Why not before?"

"We're witches," Micki said. "And we recently were contacted by Rosemary when we arrived on Paisley Island to help bring her killer to justice. Who was with you that night?"

The man laughed. Even sick and weak, it sounded evil. "Derek. Ah, Derek, I haven't thought of him in a year of Sundays. He was such a goody two shoes."

"Where is he now?" Samantha asked.

"Out there," he said nodding his head toward the window.

"Buried in the forest?" Georgia asked.

"No, sweetheart, out there," he said pointing to the horizon. "Fish food. They're gone. All of them. You look out there and see beauty; I see my own personal burial ground."

"All your books," Georgia said. "Every one of them is an account of some horrible thing you did, isn't it? There is nothing creative in that mind. You had to act out the horrors to be able to write about them, didn't you?"

"Got proof, lady?" he asked.

"No. Only that you helped Grand bury her. Can you tell me why?"

"Would you change your mind if you knew that Nellie hired her to replace you when you went to college?" Jack asked.

"No. It wouldn't change my mind in the least," Georgia said. "That's no reason to kill someone. Do you even know why you did it?"

"She was pregnant," he began saying.

"OMG," I said. "You killed her because you knocked her up?"

"No. It wasn't mine. But I would have raised it as if it was. She was in love with him, the old coot. I tried to convince her that he wouldn't be there for her, he couldn't be there for her. He was old enough to be her grandfather."

"Who?" Samantha asked. "We were under the impression she had no family."

"She didn't. I always thought that's why she fell in love with Nestor. She was an orphan who barely remembered her parents and didn't recall ever having grandparents."

"Nestor? My grandfather?" Georgia questioned.

"Yeah. He met her working in a department store. He sent her to Nellie to work for her and be a companion. But then when she discovered she was pregnant, she feared Nellie would discover the relationship and not want her. She was conflicted to be sure, but she loved them both. It was an accident. I didn't mean to hurt her. She's the only person I ever truly loved."

"That's why you buried her instead of tossing her in the ocean?" I asked.

"Yeah," he said. "I'm sorry I can't bury you. I just don't have the strength anymore, and Bruce, well, he doesn't like to spend that much time on things. Besides, they say I'll be dead in a week or two, and then this place most likely will be for sale. A fresh grave would be hard to miss."

"Who is Bruce?" Georgia asked.

"I'm Bruce," said a big surly man standing behind us. "I take care of Mr. Jack. Now I take care of you, like all the others."

Chapter Nineteen

We turned to see a man who was built like a bouncer standing behind us. My first thought was that it was going to be hard for even him to take control of the three of us. Until I saw the gun. All of my hastily formed escape plans went out the window.

The room seemed to shrink as Bruce's imposing presence filled the space. His eyes were cold and calculating as he assessed the situation in front of him.

"Jack, tell him to stand down," Georgia demanded, her voice wavering slightly.

Jack looked at Bruce and then back to Georgia. "I'm sorry, Georgia. I don't think I can do that."

As Bruce menacingly approached us, his hand waved a gun in a motion telling us to move together. Georgia glanced nervously at the rest of us. She seemed to be trying to convey that she was sorry. Sorry for bringing us into this mess. We apparently were powerful witches, but we didn't yet possess the skill, if we ever would, to stop a bullet. We needed a plan, and fast.

Just then, Sage, my owl familiar, soared into the room through an open window. Her keen eyes assessed the situation, and she seemed to understand the danger we were in. With a determined tilt of her head, she swooped toward the gun-wielding Bruce.

Bruce raised the gun, his finger hovered over the trigger, but Sage was too quick for him. She flapped her wings powerfully, diving and swooping around his head, narrowly dodging his attempts to swat her away. Her sudden appearance and agile movements disoriented him, causing his aim to falter.

Seizing the opportunity, Samantha whispered, "Now's our chance. We need to disarm him and restrain him."

Micki nodded and reached into her bag, pulling out a small vial of a powder she had created using her knowledge of herbs and potions. "This should do the trick," she said, unscrewing the cap.

With a quick, coordinated move, Micki tossed the powder into Bruce's face while Georgia and Samantha lunged forward to grab his arms, to prevent him from firing the gun. I barreled forward bent at the waist doing my best bull impersonation and hit him head on in the gut. He dropped to the floor and as the powder took effect, Bruce's eyes fluttered, his body went limp, and the gun slipped from his grasp.

We quickly secured Bruce's hands and feet with bandaging tape we found on a table next to Jack's hospital bed, ensuring he wouldn't pose a threat when he awoke from his stupor.

Sage, having done her part, landed gracefully on my shoulder, watching the scene with a wise, knowing gaze. I stroked Sage's feathers gently, whispering, "Thank you, Sage. You saved us."

With Bruce restrained and the danger averted, we had to decide what to do next.

"I don't know how long Micki's powder will keep him out, but I don't imagine that tape will last long once it does," I said. "What are we going to do now?"

"We should call the police," Samantha said.

"And tell them what exactly?" I asked. "Hello officer, we are uninvited guests at the home of one of your community's most loved celebrities, and when we accused him of murder, one we can't prove by the way unless you believe in mediums, his bodyguard tried to kill us."

"When you say it like that ..." Samantha said.

"I'm so sorry," Georgia said. "I should never have let you all come with me and put you in this situation."

"Don't be a nincompoop," Micki said. "You didn't force us to come, and we wouldn't have let you come alone."

"Besides, if you had," I reasoned, "Bruce would have fed you to the fishes because Sage would have been back on the island where I was. The way I see it, ole Jack here is not going to pay for the crimes he committed. He's all but out the door anyway. It would be nice if we could help the families understand what happened to them. We don't know who all his victims are, or what really happened to any of them, except that they became story fodder for one sick man. Our problem is Bruce. Does he know who we are and how to find us?"

Jack coughed like the dying man he was and then managed to say with a weak breath, "He doesn't. It's best if you just leave now. If you call the cops, Georgia, you're going to be in a world of snoop poop you can't imagine."

We all ignored him.

"The potion I threw on him will likely erase his memory from just before it hit him," Micki said. "But I can't be sure what he might have heard before he came in here."

"In that case," I said, "maybe we should make like ghosts and disappear! Sage, how do you feel about riding in a car?"

"Wait," Georgia said. "I mean, I need more answers. You gals can get out of here if you want. Jack, why would calling the cops cause me concerns? That doesn't make sense."

"For most of my life, I never thought of my own mortality. I guess I figured maybe I wasn't mortal. Anyway, when I got this [expletive] diagnosis, I realized for the first time, really, that I have no one. I needed to make a will because without one, in Massachusetts, with no living parents, spouse, or offspring, the great state would get it all. I have accumulated a vast fortune with my success, and the state wouldn't do anything good with it. That's when I thought of you. I figured that you at least would find some worthy place to use it. So I left it all to you. And if you call the cops while I'm on my deathbed and then they find out you stand to inherit it all ... well, you see where I'm going with this, don't you? You know

I always liked you, but you're just a small-town librarian with an overactive imagination. How do you think that's all going to play out?"

Georgia looked to Samantha. "Grand trusted you not only with her estate, but with clearing her name too. I'm going to trust you now. What should we do here? I know as an attorney, you want justice served." She pointed to the man lying in the bed with a shaking index finger, "That man has no remorse. I can tell he's not capable. No law is going to fix this. Not any of it. What do you think we should do?"

"Jack," Samantha said. "I think we've all figured out that you really don't have a wild and dark imagination. But if you help us, we will bury that secret with you. Each of your books tells the story of something that really happened, right? Do you have an accounting anywhere of who the real victims are and where their bodies are?"

"Yes," Jack said and then coughed. I had to admit with each fit it sounded worse and worse. "But it won't be easy. You girls fancy yourself as sleuths. The clues are all there. I thank the dearly departed by their first name in my acknowledgements. Something like, a special thank you to Rosemary. Without her, this story wouldn't have been possible. Then I always thank the municipality where the crime happened for hosting me during my research. Within the pages, there lie clues as to where the body is buried, so to speak. I do favor the water. Short of that, you are on your own. Just do something good with the money, will you?"

I had questions. So many questions. But I feared our time here was short. Bruce's fingers were beginning to twitch. I decided to go with the most personal, and by that, I mean to save my own hide, question in case it was my last. "How much does Bruce actually know? He said he would take care of us like the others. Did he help you? Was he your clean-up guy?"

Jack's eyes were blinking slowly, heavily, like he was struggling to stay awake. He took a deep breath, coughed some more, and then said, "No. He only kept trespassers away from the estate. It was a running joke between us that he turned them into fish food. He loved The Godfather movies and always wanted to be a connected man. But that brute is pure mush on the inside. That gun isn't real. It's a set prop from one of my movies. He can't hurt anyone or anything. He probably would be concerned that the people I did leave for fish food weren't healthy for the slimy little creatures. He's harmless. You're safe. Now get out of here and let me die alone. You know it's what I deserve. And Georgia, I'm sorry. As sorry as I'm capable of being."

"Well, bless your pea pickin' little heart," Georgia said.

"Y'all!" I said pointing to where Bruce was lying in the floor, "We need to go. Now!" It was no longer just his fingers twitching. He was waking up.

"Jack just told us he was harmless," Georgia said. That woman possessed the most compassion of anyone I'd ever met.

"Really, Georgia? Do you trust that man with your life?" I asked. "Now that you know the real man? Cause I don't."

"Point well made!" Samantha said. "Let's ride, witches!"

Chapter Twenty

Bruce was starting to wake up. We didn't even say goodbye to Jack. Once we cleared the front door, Sage flew off my shoulder and landed on the roof of our rental car.

"Phoebe, I'm tired," the owl explained when we reached the car. "It may take me a day or two to return to the island."

"I was serious when I asked how you felt about riding in a car," I said.

"But we flew here on a plane," Samantha said.

"Can we just get in the car and drive out of here?" Micki asked opening a rear passenger door. "We can figure it all out any place but here."

"Come on Sage, it's not too bad riding in a car," Georgia said. "Venus doesn't love it, but I bet you're brave enough."

"I will, but it's mostly because I need to know what you ladies are doing," Sage said. "It's my job, you know."

We piled into the car, and when I say Georgia drove like the hounds of hell were after us, I'm not exaggerating one little bit. Once we hit the main highway, she slowed down, and all of us took a collective deep breath.

Samantha in the front passenger seat spoke first. "Micki, what are the chances that Bruce won't even remember we were there or anything about us?"

"It's possible," she answered. "But honestly, I don't know what the actual probability is. Since we aren't there, he may have no reason to think about it. So maybe it will just never come to mind. Then again, he might. The only way we could know for sure is if we had stayed, and that didn't seem like a good idea at all."

"I agree." Samantha said. "If we aren't there when he wakes up, why would he think about us? Now, we just need to figure out the best way to get back home."

"We could just keep the rental car and drive back," Georgia said. "That way, Sage wouldn't have to fly all that way again."

"Thank you, Georgia, that's very kind of you," I answered. I looked at Sage, who was sitting on the backseat between me and Micki. She was sound asleep. "I just realized that not only did she fly the whole way, she's been awake all day, when she normally sleeps."

"That's a long drive, ladies!" Samantha said. "I'm due in court the day after tomorrow and I really need some time to prep. I've totally ignored my job since Nellie walked into my office, and I can't keep doing that, even if hanging out with you all is more fun."

"Well, I don't suppose teleporting is actually a thing, is it?" Georgia asked looking at Micki in the rearview mirror.

"Some say it is," she answered. "But I've never been able to make it happen. You know what? I have an idea that could work!"

"Put Samantha on a plane and the rest of us drive?" I asked.

"That could work too," Georgia acknowledged.

"Not what I was thinking," Micki said. "Layla is the answer. Remember Layla from Sentinel Security, the one who can manipulate time? Except for this rental car, think back to everything you can remember from the time we left the island this morning. Did anyone have any interactions with anyone along the way? We need to make sure we wouldn't be disrupting the time continuum. Then we can call and ask if it's possible. Maybe she could return us to before the trip at all if the only people we interacted with were Jack and Bruce. We might be able to remember what happened, but no one could prove we were there. And then we would be back in plenty of time for Samantha's court date."

"Brilliant!" I said, giddy that we might be able to reclaim this time and remove all evidence of the trip.

"We interacted with the check-in officer at the airport in Wilmington," Samantha said.

"And that brings up a good point," Micki said. "Who used a charge card anywhere along the way?"

"I used a card to pay for the tickets, of course," Georgia said. "I booked the no-contact rental car on a card too."

"Those could be explained. If we roll back time, and we never board the plane, it would be like we missed the flight, right?" I asked. "But how do we explain the missing rental car?"

"Could anyone prove that we are the ones who picked it up?" Georgia asked.

"Cameras." Samantha said. "You know that airports and especially those rental lots are covered in them. We are four fairly identifiable women. And we weren't trying to hide our identity."

"You ladies are missing the point, I think," Micki said. "If we return in time to before the trip, and we don't take the trip, then it never happened. We need to talk to Layla to be sure. Samantha, can you call her?"

I found myself stroking Sage in the backseat; I was missing my little dog. I was happy to have this wise familiar to help me in my new journey, but I really missed Harper Lee. When I left Texas, I hadn't imagined that I would be gone forever. I didn't really want to leave to go get her, though I needed my car, my stuff, and my dog. As I was trying to figure out various ways I could get them all here without having to spend days on the road, I totally missed the conversation going on around me in the car.

Georgia, Samantha, and Micki all whooped in celebration, and when they did, they startled me out of my own personal conundrum, and Sage awake from her slumber. We both looked around to see what the fuss was about.

"I'm sorry, y'all. I zoned out for a bit there. What's happening?"

"Layla confirmed that she can help us transport back to before the trip," Micki said.

"Without any residual issues," Samantha added.

"And we will still remember what we learned in Nantucket," Georgia said. "We won't have any proof of what Jack admitted, but he'll probably die before we get back to North Carolina anyway."

"I do have proof," Samantha said. "But I assume it will disappear too. I recorded the conversations while we were there. But if the trip is erased, so will the recording; is that correct, Micki?"

"I believe so. That would make sense," the wise witch answered.

"Alrighty then," Georgia said. "Looks like we have a sixteen-hour drive ahead of us. How do we want to do this? Find a hotel for the night and start fresh in the morning, or drive until we can't drive and then stop?"

"I say let's keep moving if we can," Samantha said as she brought up navigation directions on the car's screen to get us back to North Carolina.

"I'm famished but otherwise happy to keep rolling," I added.

"If we can keep moving until a little after midnight, we will be on the other side of New York," Samantha said. "I think going through the B Apple at night is preferable, don't you think?"

"With four of us to share the driving, I think that makes a lot of sense," Georgia said. "Once we get off the ferry, we can get fast food and keep rolling. It's not as though we don't have enough to talk about."

"I know there are more important things," I said, "and maybe this is just me, because for as long as I can remember, I have dreamed of being an author. But is anyone else really disturbed by all of this?"

"By all of this, do you mean finding out we are witches?" Georgia asked, "Inheriting not one, but two estates? Taking a two-day road trip with an owl in the car? Or the fact that one of the world's most beloved authors is a fake, a hack, a psychopath?"

"Well, yes. But at the moment, what I'm wrestling with most is what Nellie said, and then Jack too," I explained. "That authors can really only write what they know. When my son was in high school and I revealed my dream to become a writer to him, he asked what I would write. I said mysteries because it's what I love to read. He answered me by saying he always wondered about the minds of the people who write them. After meeting Jack, it appears maybe he was right. I'm feeling very disillusioned right now, confused, and frankly, I'm worried."

"Phoebe, dear," Micki said as the only true fiction author in the car, "we are all nothing but a collection of our experiences. And as authors, those experiences absolutely influence what we write. But we don't have to live something to experience it. Think about it this way. We learn from the books we read, from the movies and television that we watch, from the news, and, not only from our own experiences, but also those of the people we know and love. I write romance because it's what I know."

"Which is exactly why I will never write romance," I interrupted. "I know nothing of the beast. Except that I don't know what happily ever after looks like."

"Don't give up too soon, my darling," Micki warned me. "The point is that we experience things not only as the doer. Sometimes we are the seer or the listener. We still experience them, and we know what they look like from our perspective."

"Thanks, that makes me feel better," I said.

"That's why I called Jack a hack and a fake. He didn't have the talent to learn through any means other than doing," Georgia explained. "I spent my entire childhood in frilly dresses and shiny Mary Janes, sitting in my Grand's study, listening to her talk to all kinds of authors. They absolutely did not have to play out or participate in the stories they wrote. Only Jack had to do that."

"With all due respect," Samantha said, "last week when the man was sitting outside your house babysitting coolers full of casseroles, you wouldn't have dreamed that Jack was a serial killer, would you?"

"Touché, to the prosecuting attorney on my right," Georgia said. "Touché."

CHAPTER TWENTY-ONE

Sixteen hours is a long drive. We stopped about every three hours and traded off the driving task. There was time for us to figure out how to spend Jack's money. The goal was to solve every case he ever wrote about and to help the families of the victims finally have closure. We wrestled over whether we should attempt to do so without destroying his name and reputation, Georgia's wish, or exposing him for the sick puppy that he was, my own desire. Samantha settled the debate by pointing out that one was not possible without the other.

Solving the puzzles at this point was not about who did it; it was about who the victims were and where the bodies were buried. Those buried at sea were not going to be recoverable and were going to be harder to prove. Lakes and land burials would give us some proof, but the only way we would get law enforcement to listen would be to tell them how we knew. And that was going to shine a spotlight on Jack Poe.

Micki wondered if, after we solved the first couple, maybe the FBI would take over. Which would be great because

I could already feel the task sucking the soul right out of me. I didn't come to Paisley Island to solve a serial killer's crimes. I came to be a writer. Well, that's not really true either. I came because I was called, I had nothing else to do, and I was promised an inheritance of some kind. I never dreamed this is where I would land.

We also talked about getting on with the development of Paisley Island. That's when I learned that Nellie's lovely house had eight bedrooms. Who knew? Not I. I realized then that I had been in a kind of altered state since the funeral. I went from my room, AKA Nellie's room, to the kitchen and back again, except for the one foray to the attic and twice in the study. Georgia wanted to invite a couple more of her author friends to come and stay and help us determine what would make the island an attractive place for authors to want to relocate. While I drove, she wrote a number of emails to be sent after we time traveled back a couple of days.

While Micki was driving, I received a phone call from my daughter, Mandy. I was just about to answer when Micki warned me not to! It was a real struggle to remember that basically anything that happened on this trip, except our memories, wouldn't actually happen in the future. Mandy left a voicemail message and I listened. She was excited to be finished with her last day of school and out for the summer. She loved her job as a kindergarten teacher. But she loved having her summers off, too. I had a great idea.

"Hey, Georgia, any chance we have an extra room available for my daughter? I would like to see if she would be willing to bring my car, my dog, and my clothes and come for a visit. I can fly her home afterwards. I mean, after all, I suppose she's a Hadley witch too, right?"

"Sure, why not! The more the merrier," Georgia said.

"I can move back to my house," Samantha said. "Maybe I can have dinner with you all each day and then go home."

"Is that really what you want to do?" I asked. "Have you considered staying on the Island permanently? I mean I know you need to get back to work, but how can you stand to miss coffee with us in the mornings, but also, I think it's kind of hysterical to have the food chain of familiars in the same place."

"You say that," Georgia said, "but I've been terrified that Venus would decide that Hazel was an intriguing snack. And I admit I've been a little worried if she should get out, if she would be in danger from Sage. I've heard stories about birds of prey swooping up cats and small dogs."

"You don't have to fear me," Sage said, waking up. "None of you have to worry about any of us. As familiars, we understand each other's roles in the lives of our witches. We can't hurt one another. Now, getting along is a whole other matter. There will be squabbles for sure, but no physical harm."

"I have thought about it off and on, a little," Samantha said. "But I love my condo, it's close to my office and the courthouse, and I'm not a writer. The island is a writer's retreat. I think I'll feel out of place."

"You aren't a writer yet," Georgia said.

"No one has asked my opinion," Micki said. "But I'll offer it anyway. You three together are going to be the most powerful witches of all time once you embrace and learn your powers. You will be called on by the universe to settle all manner of matters. The closer you are in proximity, the easier that will be to do. You don't all have to live next door to each other, but over time, I suspect you're going to want to live close."

"How important is your legal career to you, Samantha?" Georgia asked. "Would you ever consider giving it up?"

"It's been everything to me," she answered. "Being an attorney is my dream, I worked hard to get where I am, and if I'm honest, I hope to be a judge someday. It's not just what I do, it's who I am. What on earth would I do if I gave it up?"

"Write!" Georgia, Micki, and I all said at once.

"Who knows," I said. "Maybe you're the next John Grisham."

"Speaking of writing," Micki said, "Phoebe, have you decided what you're going to write?"

"I'm going to tell Rosemary's story," I said, in a fictional account, of course. "It will be a mystery, I suppose. Then we'll see what happens."

As Georgia drove across the bridge that connected Paisley Island to the quaint little town of Lansbury, I had an odd sensation of it being some type of portal. A portal that separated what happened on the island from the rest of the world. I had a fleeting idea about how wonderful it would be if we could totally isolate the island from everyday life. Could we make it a Utopia where we could escape the mainland's news, drama, and trauma?

"Look alive, ladies, we're almost home!" Georgia said.

"Whoa, stop the car! Please, can you stop the car?" Sage said from the backseat.

Georgia crammed the brakes, brought the car to a stop, and asked, "What's wrong?"

"If the other wildlife on the island see me arriving in a car, I will never live it down. I need to get out now. Thanks for the ride, though."

I opened my door and Sage walked across my lap to the open door. Her wings were too wide to open in the car.

"Would you like for me to pick you up and set you down so you can open your wings?" I asked her.

"No, no, I've got this," the bird said. But she just sat there on my lap looking out the door. "Well, actually, I don't have this. It's alright if you want to pick me up, I suppose. It gives me the willies, but I'll be fine. Thank you," she said as I gently lifted her and set her on the road.

"It's a good thing there isn't any traffic on this bridge," I said. Sage flew away and Georgia proceeded to the island.

"How can you be so chipper?" Samantha asked scrolling on her phone.

"I'm so tired I'm back here having fantasies and delusions of converting the island into a compound instead of a retreat," I confessed.

"You mean like a prepper community, with off-grid living?" Samantha asked.

"You know," Micki said, "A lot of people are feeling the need to withdraw from life as we've come to know it. The politics, the religious debates, the chasm between generations, and the violence, are spawning compounds all over the country. Why can't we have an author's compound? A mystical author's compound. We can set our own laws. Of course, I'm sitting here talking like I'm one of you. I realize I'm not an owner here, but I know I'm thrilled by the prospect of moving to the island. It would be the best if we only had to leave it when we wanted to venture out into this new wild world."

"You are one of us," Georgia said. "An honorary one of us, but one, nonetheless. And I hate to burst y'alls bubbles; but, we're going to have to leave now and again to buy food. The island just isn't big enough to build a subdivision, a retail outlet that only a few residents couldn't support, and/or a farm to grow our food. Besides, I can't survive without my red and white meats."

Georgia glided to a stop at the recently established guard shack at the entrance to Paisley Island. Layla was waiting for us at the cute little building at the end of the bridge from the mainland.

Georgia rolled down her window and Layla approached. "Did we miss anything while we were gone?" she asked.

"Nothing you won't be able to experience firsthand," Layla answered cryptically.

"I don't know if I like the sound of that," Samantha said. "It's the devil we know versus the devil we don't. If we go back in time, we don't know what awaits us here."

"And you can't tell us?" I asked Layla.

"No, ma'am. I can't tell you. If you were supposed to know what happens in the future, you would know."

"Someone remind me why we need to go back in time," Georgia asked.

"Because Samantha has to be in court early tomorrow morning and hasn't prepared," I said.

"And to erase our presence in Nantucket. In case it's ever brought into question," Micki said.

"We didn't do anything wrong back there," Georgia argued.

"Except take off with a rental car," Samantha reminded us.

"Oh, fiddle dee dee, that's easily fixed with a credit card," Georgia said.

"I should probably share with you that, if there isn't a compelling reason to go back in time, you probably shouldn't do it. Even if you think you've thought it through, well, you could miss a ripple."

"Let's take a vote," Georgia said. "All in favor of going back in time raise your hand."

Only Samantha raised her hand. "Oh, fine," she said. "It will be the first time I show up for court without my homework done."

"Maybe you can request a continuance," Layla said.

"On what grounds? I can't use the dog ate my homework. We don't have a dog," she said.

"I do," I said. "And I'm missing her terribly, no offense to Sage. Harper Lee doesn't talk to me, she's not interested in helping me on any journey, and she definitely isn't big enough to eat homework, but I do miss my little friend."

"So you aren't going back in time?" Layla asked.

"No, I don't suppose we are, the majority has spoken," Samantha said. "But just see if I ever trust you three in a pinch again."

"In that case, I can tell you that you have guests waiting for you," Layla said.

"Guests? Who? I never sent the emails," Georgia asked.

"The police chief has come calling. I told him you should be back from your errands about now."

"What on earth, now?" Samantha said.

Layla just turned and went back inside the guard shack. I wondered if she was upset that we chose not to travel back in time. But I too was more concerned about what the chief wanted.

Chapter Twenty-Two

Talk about being conflicted. As we wound around the paved path to the front of Hadley Manor, sure enough, the driveway in front of the house was occupied by two cars. Just as Layla had warned us, the police chief himself was there. But before I could be concerned about what the law wanted on our little island, I saw a mirage. I shook my head, certain that fatigue was playing tricks on me.

"Does anyone else see..." I started saying, but I was interrupted by Georgia.

"Is that a pink VW Beetle?"

"Yes, yes, it is!" I declared. "It's my midlife crisis I expressed when my youngest left for college. It has pink club plaid upholstery," I said as we drove past the car with my forehead touching the window to see who was in the car. "And my daughter, Mandy!"

Georgia stopped the car, and I scrambled out of the backseat as fast as I could. When she saw me, Mandy got out of my car. And in her arms was my precious, tiny but mighty, teacup Maltese, Harper Lee. The dog yipped and jumped into my arms, bathed me with kisses and then took to her perch on my shoulder. Little thing that she was, she started holding on to my shoulder with her front paws and riding there like a parrot when she was still a puppy. To this day, it was still her favorite mode of transportation. With Harper Lee settled, Mandy then gave me a cautious hug designed to not disturb the dog.

"What are you doing here?" I asked.

"I tried to call and let you know," Mandy explained. "At first, I was hoping to surprise you, and then I got cold feet. But you didn't answer, so surprise! I thought you could use your car, Harper Lee, and some clothes. Since school's out, I decided to take a road trip to see this private island my mom inherited."

"That's so thoughtful of you! I was planning to call you and invite you to come when we got back from an impromptu trip," I said. "I'm sorry I missed your call. We must have been in a dead zone or something," and cringed at my own pun. "There's so much I want to share with you. I've learned important things about us, and it's going to affect you too, especially since you were born in 1993," I said rambling.

Georgia, Samantha, and Micki walked up behind me, and I introduced Mandy and Harper Lee.

"Shall we go see what Chief wants with us?" Samantha asked.

The five of us walked toward the front of the Manor. The Chief of the Lansbury police department seemed right at home in a rocking chair on the front porch.

"Good afternoon, ladies. It's a fine day out here, don't you think?"

"It is, indeed, Chief Taylor," Georgia said. "What can we do for you today?"

"I wanted to come by and tell you personally that the fine district attorney has accepted the journal entry confession of one George Govender, III, AKA Gordy Govender, as true and thereby is dropping all charges against Miss Nellie," he said.

"Well, thank you for that. It's a relief to be sure," Georgia said.

"What about Gordy, Chief?" Samantha asked. "Has that case been solved?"

"Well, we have a person of interest. That young lady that arrived on the island with him has disappeared. The name she gave us was a fake name. The address doesn't exist. But we'll find her sooner or later. We believe she killed him, but we don't have a motive."

"What was the cause of death?" Georgia asked.

"To be honest, the coroner couldn't find one. The working theory is he was drugged or poisoned with something that stopped his heart. Something that wouldn't show up in his system. The crime scene techs found some blood on a boulder next to the lake. He was found not far from there. We believe he was impaired, fell, hit his head, stumbled a bit, and then collapsed."

"Maybe we should consider filling in that lake," Georgia mumbled. "Forgive our manners, we would invite you in for a glass of lemonade, but the girls and I just returned from a long road trip and aren't prepared for company."

"No need, and thank you for your kindness," Chief Taylor said, "I also wanted to mention that there are rumors floating around Lansbury that you plan to develop the island into a community of some sort, build a subdivision, or something? If that's the case, the city may need to consider incorporating the island to offer you police, fire, and other services and protections."

"No doubt that would increase your tax base as well," Samantha said.

"Well, of course, we have to pay for those services. It will probably mean we need to add officers to cover the extra land and population," the chief said.

"Spoken like a true politician," Samantha said, grinning and patting the chief on the shoulder.

"The ladies and I were just talking about that," Micki said. "We're thinking of having a private police department for the island. So all that won't be necessary."

"I see," the chief said. "Well, as you know, Lansbury is a small town without much crime, so to speak. Some of our officers might be inclined to work some extra hours for you. And if I can be of any assistance, let me know. But remember that you are required to get planning and building permits and inspections. Even a private island is part of the county and state. You can't privatize that."

"Thanks, Chief," Samantha said. "I'm here to make sure that everything is done by the book. Please tell your wife that we appreciate her sending you out here to deliver the news about Nellie. It would be so nice if we could pull back all those slanderous news reports of her arrest. A press conference dropping the charges would be a nice gesture, though Heaven knows it won't get the same amount of coverage. And I assure you we will be contacting the Inspections Department as soon as we finalize our plans. We're just beginning to sort everything out. Not only are we coping with our grief from losing Nellie, but we just came from saying goodbye to an old family friend who is also dying. Now, if you'll excuse us, we need to tend to our own matters."

"Yes, ma'am. Y'all have a good evening, now. I'll see about that press release," he said, walking back to his car.

"I said conference, Andrew, not a release. We all know a piece of paper will be ignored," Samantha said.

"Yes, ma'am. I'll get right on that," he said, opening the door of his car and sliding in as quickly as his pudgy belly would allow.

Once through the door of the manor, the women burst into laughter.

"Seriously, Samantha, I really think you need to move to the island too," Georgia said. "We need that kind of no-nonsense approach. And Micki, a private police department? Really?"

"I think we can apply to get Sentinel Security appointed as our private law enforcement," Samantha said. "It's really a brilliant idea. I'll check into the process after my court appearance tomorrow."

"Wait, wait," Mandy said. "Are you serious? The chief of police is Andrew Taylor? Like Andy Taylor?"

"Fun fact," Georgia said. "Mount Airy, North Carolina was Andy Griffith's hometown and was the basis for Mayberry in the show. It turns out that the Taylors have been the royal law enforcement family there for generations. Our Andrew—he hates being called Andy—has a twin brother. Alex got the job of chief of police. and Andrew moved out of town to seek other opportunities. He didn't want to work for his brother."

"Well, bless his heart," we all said at once.

"Dibs on the first shower," Samantha called and raced up the stairs.

"I need to check on Venus," Georgia said and also went upstairs.

"I'm going to see if Nancy and Cindy need any help getting dinner on the table," Micki said, leaving Mandy and me still standing in the foyer.

"Come on in, let's go to the kitchen. Do you need something to drink?" I asked my daughter.

"What I need is a restroom," she said crossing her legs and bouncing.

"It's right over there. You said you brought clothes for me? I'll go get them out of the car," I said. "Keep Harper Lee with you. Georgia has a big cat and I'm not sure how she feels about dogs. When I get back, I'll explain about us being witches."

"Wait, what?"

"Don't wet your pants, missy, we can discuss this at length in a few minutes."

CHAPTER TWENTY - THREE

I struggled with the heavy suitcase as I made my way towards the front door of Hadley Manor. After a grueling two-day road trip, all I wanted was a shower, food, a visit with Mandy, snuggles with Harper Lee, and a good night's sleep. But as I approached the door, two sleek sports cars pulled up, and two men stepped out of them.

"Hey there, gorgeous," one of the men said, flashing me a charming smile. "I'm Kelly, and this is my friend Davis. We heard about the author community you're building here, and we thought we'd check it out."

I felt my frustration mount. The last thing we needed was uninvited guests showing up at our doorstep. Especially today of all days. But I tried to keep my manners in check and put on a polite smile.

"Well, I'm sorry to say that we're not really set up for visitors yet," I said, hoping to discourage them from sticking around.

Kelly's smile didn't waver. "That's okay. We're not exactly looking for a five-star hotel. We just want to see what all the fuss is about. I already see an inspiring view and a potential muse."

I felt a pang of annoyance at his casual dismissal of my efforts, but I tried to hide it behind a veneer of charm.

"Well, I suppose we could give you a tour, but I can't guarantee much in the way of amenities," I said, hoping to make them see reason. "The cafe isn't even built, let alone opened. But we still have funeral casseroles in the freezer."

Kelly's eyes sparkled with amusement. "I'm sure we'll manage. And who knows, maybe we'll even find some inspiration for our next books."

Davis chimed in, "It's perfect. Survival on a private island inhabited by magical wordsmith geeks."

I rolled my eyes. "Yeah, because there's nothing like a bunch of witches and ghosts to get the creative juices flowing."

"That's me," Davis said. "Killin' 'em with words. Don't mind my friend Kelly here. He's a born-again flirt. But we aren't bad guys. I promise."

Kelly chuckled. "I like your sense of humor, Phoebe. Maybe we can work on a project together. What do you write?"

I felt a flutter in my stomach at the thought of collaborating with another author. But I was still miffed at the uninvited intrusion. Besides, I was just thinking about being an author and I wasn't ready to talk to a stranger about what I was or wasn't writing.

"I'm sorry, Kelly, but we're really not set up for guests yet," I said, hoping he would take the hint.

Kelly's smile faltered for a moment, but then he leaned in closer. "Okay, I'll make a deal with you. If you let us stay, I'll buy you a drink, and we can talk about our favorite books."

I felt my resolve weakening. I was tired and hungry, and the thought of a glass of wine was tempting. But I didn't want to be seen as a pushover.

"I don't know, Kelly. I'm not sure you can afford my tastes," I said, giving him a teasing grin.

Kelly chuckled. "I think I can manage. And who knows, maybe we'll even become friends."

The front door opened, and Micki stuck her head out and looked around. "There you are!" she said and rushed out the door. I thought she was looking for me, but she rushed right past me and to the men and hugged them both. "I see you met Phoebe."

"We actually haven't been properly introduced," I said. "I assume you knew they were coming, then."

"Well, I'm happy to do the honors," Micki said. "Phoebe, this is Kelly Keaton and Davis Ingram. Gentlemen, this is Phoebe Ellis."

I became aware my mouth was wide open as I stared at one of my all-time favorite thriller authors, Kelly Keaton. It was a testament to my fatigue that I didn't recognize him at first, because once Micki said his name, I couldn't unsee the man who looked exactly like the photo on the back of his book covers. I closed my mouth, hearing in my mind my grandmother telling me to close my mouth before a fly flew in. I dropped the suitcase and offered a hand.

"Well, why didn't you tell me that you're that Kelly? And that Davis? It's a pleasure to meet you!" I said.

"Let's go inside. We've got a light dinner ready."

"We heard!" Kelly said. "Hadley Manor is serving their famous Funeral Casserole tonight. It's my favorite. And I brought a wine perfect for the pairing."

"On a day like today," I said, "any wine will do!"

After getting everyone settled into guest rooms and a wonderful night of dreamless sleep, I awoke refreshed and excited the next day. It seemed this little dream of Nellie's was really going to happen, and I couldn't be more excited to be a part of it. I woke up and took the red leather journal out onto the balcony and sat with Harper Lee in my lap and Sage on the railing and wrote about Rosemary for an hour before joining the others downstairs.

We had decided the night before that we needed to have a meeting of the familiars. We knew it was going to take three to six months to build the houses and have the island ready for move-ins, even with magical assistance. We were hoping to have an island celebration for Samhain, the Celtic new year, when the veil between the worlds was the thinnest. It was commonly called Halloween and the Day of the Dead. But that meant that for a while Hazel the hedgehog, Venus the cat, Sage the owl, and my little Harper Lee were going to have to coexist in the same house. When I closed the journal, I spoke to Sage.

"Sage, we're planning for all the familiars to meet again today to be introduced to Harper Lee because we're all going to be living here for a while. Would you like to join us?"

"Hi, Sage, I'm Harper Lee. This is my mom. Will you swoop down and eat me?"

"Harper Lee! Since when can you talk?" I exclaimed.

"I've always been able to talk," my little white fluffball said. "You just didn't think you could hear me. You thought you were making up conversations with me and imagining my responses, but actually I was communicating with you telepathically."

"Well, I'll be a monkey's uncle! Who knew?"

"We did," Sage and Harper Lee said at the same time.

"Well, then, let's go downstairs for you to meet the others, my talking dog."

Downstairs everyone was gathered around the huge dining room table where we'd had dinner last night. Our little group had more than doubled since I arrived. Harper Lee and I were the last to arrive, but Kelly was just ahead of me. Nancy and Cindy were sitting at the table with the others and pointed to a rolling butler's tray with a thermal coffee carafe, mugs, and cream and sugar.

"Good morning," I said, and Kelly turned to look at me.

"It is now," he said. I felt the blush creeping in even while questioning if I could believe anything he said.

He never took his eyes off me, but his hand reached out towards the mugs, and he grabbed a handle. "Can I buy you a cup of coffee?"

"You know, Kelly. I'm not the kinda girl who can be bought," I said, noticing that the mug he was holding wasn't empty. I was biting my lip determined not to laugh and give it away.

"Okay, well, if you insist, I'll fix it for myself," he said and looked down in time to see Hazel stick her little rodent looking nose out of the top of the mug. His reaction was exactly the same as mine when it first happened to me. He tossed the mug in the air in surprise and then scrambled to catch it. The only difference was that I too tried to catch the poor critter. We bumped hands and then recoiled from a charge of electricity that shocked us both. He recovered before I did and laid his hand flat on the ground and caught the mug as it hit the floor. Once everyone knew Hazel was safe, the silence in the room erupted into gales of laughter.

"I watched that all happen in slow motion!" Mandy said between fits of laughter.

"I say, that is quite enough!" Hazel said from inside the mug. I swear I could see her quills shivering. "I do not enjoy being your practical joke. Oh, what is that?"

I looked to see what Hazel was looking at and was surprised to see it was Harper Lee sitting by my foot.

"Good morning, Hazel. I'm so sorry we almost dropped you," I said. "This is my dog, Harper Lee. I've had her for three years, and I just learned this morning that she can talk."

"That's a dog?" Hazel said her eyes wider than I'd ever seen them.

"Don't laugh," Harper Lee said.

"Not laughing!" Hazel said. "Finally, an animal not big enough to swallow me whole. Right? Are you a carnivore?"

"I don't know what a carnivore is, but I wouldn't eat you. I just eat kibble and tacos. I really like tacos."

"Cool! Is she staying?" Hazel asked looking at me.

"As long as I do, at least," I answered.

"Wanna be my bestie?" Hazel asked Harper Lee.

"Hey, I thought I'm your bestie!" Samantha protested.

"Nah, you're my hooman and my witch. Those are good relationships, but my bestie should be an animal, don't you think?" Hazel explained and turned back to Harper Lee.

Just then Venus leaped from her throne, also known as Georgia's lap.

"I don't understand this besties business," Venus said. Then she noticed Harper Lee. "That. That's what you're calling a dog? She's a puppy, right? She's going to grow, isn't she?"

"Yes, she's a ..."

"I can speak for myself," Harper Lee said, cutting me off, "I'm a teacup Maltese, one of the cutest dog breeds out there. My size is perfect for snuggling in my owner's lap, and my soft, white fur makes me look like a living stuffed animal. I'm a charming and lovable dog who brings joy and laughter to everyone around me. I may be small, but I have a big personality and a heart full of love."

I stood there staring at my little fluff ball. "And can hold her own against creatures great and small," I added.

"Well, isn't that a fine how do you do. I'm Venus. Judging by your voice, your bark won't be too annoying and you're small enough to be easily ignored. I think you'll be okay."

"I'm better than okay. You're beautiful, Venus. On the outside anyway. And, well, you can't help the cat part. Did somebody say something about breakfast? I'm famished!"

EPILOGUE

The days flew by in a blur. Mandy and I had the best talks of our lives while walking Harper Lee around the island and talking about what it all meant to be Hadley witches, authors, and living in a closed community like the one we were planning. I learned that she was dating someone and seemed very happy with her job teaching kindergarten in Texas. But she did ask if she could come visit on school breaks, and that warmed my heart immensely. She wanted to learn more about being a Hadley witch. I was pleased she was open to explore and fascinated by the idea.

Samantha managed to wrangle enough commitments from contractors, plumbers, and electricians from four surrounding counties to help us build the houses. Micki, Kelly, and Davis all agreed to stay and help keep things on track. We were going to take a barn raising type approach to the houses. We would each be responsible for two houses, our own and one other. Nancy and Cindy would work with Georgia to get the carriage house cafe built, and Micki found a gifted landscape architect to create a park-like community garden in the center of the island.

I was continuing to write the fictionalized account of Rosemary and her short life. Kelly read the first chapters and said it was a great start. Over time I learned that Kelly wasn't so much a flirt as someone who really respected and admired women. He was complimentary, supportive, and understanding. But no one is that perfect. I secretly took it as my own personal challenge to discover his fatal flaw. I suspected he might have been doing the same with me.

Georgia decided to commission three sculptures for the gardens. One of the three original Hadley witches, one of Nellie, Georgia, and Rosemary, and the third of Georgia, Samantha, and me. We were embracing the power and number of three like it was a jackpot winning lottery number. It turned out that Davis was an exceptional artist, and he created sketches of Rosemary from my descriptions as I had seen her in my dreams, then using photos of the others, created the draft to give the sculptures of what we wanted. Micki said that was going to work out famously with the garden design. For now, she was keeping that close to the vest. It was a surprise, she said.

In the evenings after dinner, we read Jack Poe's books and made copious notes of the potential clues. Georgia decided to sell his house on Nantucket, auction off all the contents, and create a fund for victims of violence and a foundation for the mentally ill.

Samantha did go through all the proper channels in the great state of North Carolina to form a Paisley Island Police, Fire, and Rescue Department. Then she hired the Sentinel Security firm to fill those roles. But we did have to still deal with the Office of Inspections. So far, the inspector assigned to our island wasn't giving us much grief, but we didn't plan to give him any reason to. He requested an x-ray scan of the subterranean ground to make sure we weren't building over any ancient burial grounds. You should have seen our faces the day he told us that. But it was only required for where we were going to build. Rosemary was buried so close to the lake that we wouldn't be building there, and we all breathed a huge sigh of relief and prayed there were no more bodies buried here we didn't know about.

Georgia, Micki, Davis, and Kelly contacted authors they knew to possess certain gifts to tell them about the island. Georgia decided she would like to live in Hadley Manor and run it like a B&B. If authors came and we liked them and felt comfortable with them, they would be invited to stay for a longer time in one of the houses. Samantha also agreed to live on the island. The more she thought about our encouragement to be the next John Grisham, the more it felt like a challenge. And Samantha never backed down from one of those.

Nancy and Cindy decided with our permission and encouragement to sell their duplex on the mainland and add on two apartments on the back of the carriage house cafe.

That meant we were looking for occupants for seven of the houses we planned to build. We would complete mine,

Samantha's, Micki's, Kelly's and Davis's first and then the rest. Once our houses were finished, we could move out of the manor and start inviting guests.

We shared with no one that the woman the police were looking for in connection to Gordy's death was a mirage, a Sentinel shifter's creation. While at first, we were still concerned about who killed him and whether or not we were in danger, Nellie appeared in all of our dreams and assured us we were safe. Gordy had killed Melanie to protect Nellie from the witch hunter. But Melanie's lover, also a witch hunter, killed Gordy. He was in fact the one who appeared as Gordy to the police and framed Nellie. But apparently, he had then been dealt with by some magical council and was no longer a threat to us. She assured us we had an entourage of protection from beyond the veil while we learned to be the most powerful witches of the twenty-first century.

It was a lovely summer. We learned, we grew, we laughed. We had dreams and visions about our special compound community. None of us foresaw what would really happen opening up our community on Paisley Island.

To be continued…

With her new magical abilities and a budding romance, Phoebe's in a good place. But when a body washes up on the beach, could she lose it all? Find out in *Witches, Fishes, & Deaths.*

To stay updated with the lastest news and extras about my books, sign up for my twice a month newsletter and claim free books.

To check out more of my cozy mysteries you can find the most up-to-date listings here:

Thanks for reading! I hope you enjoyed the story. I'd love to get to know you through my newsletter or Facebook group. But if you'd rather just stalk from afar, that's okay too. You can follow me on Amazon or BookBub. To join the Facebook group scan and join!